DEVIL'S BARGAIN

"Hello, Fargo, you son of a gun," Blue Raven said, swaying slightly from the liquor he'd been drinking. "I've struck a good bargain with my friend here, Chief Iron Tail. Would you like to hear?"

"No," Skye snarled.

"I'll tell you anyway," Blue Raven said. "I get ten of his best horses, four rifles, ammunition, and whiskey for a month." Blue Raven smiled. "And guess what he gets? The blonde. Your pinto. And you."

"Me?" said Skye.

Blue Raven nodded. "The Bloods are holding a special celebration tonight and you'll be guest of honor. Of course, you'll be tied to stakes during the festivities. But you won't mind so much by the time they're done skinning you alive."

So this was it, Skye Fargo thought. The end of the trail for the Trailsman. . . .

THE
TRAILSMAN
120

WYOMING MANHUNT

by

Jon Sharpe

A SIGNET BOOK

SIGNET
Published by the Penguin Group
Penguin Books USA Inc., 375 Hudson Street,
New York, New York, 10014, U.S.A.
Penguin Books Ltd, 27 Wrights Lane, London W8 5TZ, England
Penguin Books Australia Ltd, Ringwood, Victoria, Australia
Penguin Books Canada Ltd, 10 Alcorn Avenue, Toronto, Ontario, Canada M4V 3B2
Penguin Books (N.Z.) Ltd, 182-190 Wairau Road,
Auckland 10, New Zealand

Penguin Books Ltd, Registered Offices:
Harmondsworth, Middlesex, England

First published by Signet, an imprint of New American Library,
a division of Penguin Books USA Inc.

First Printing, December, 1991

10 9 8 7 6 5 4 3 2 1

The first chapter of this book previously appeared in *Renegade Rifles*,
the one hundred nineteenth volume in this series.

 REGISTERED TRADEMARK—MARCA REGISTRADA

PRINTED IN THE UNITED STATES OF AMERICA

The Trailsman

Beginnings . . . they bend the tree and they mark the man. Skye Fargo was born when he was eighteen. Terror was his midwife, vengeance his first cry. Killing spawned Skye Fargo, ruthless, cold-blooded murder. Out of the acrid smoke of gunpowder still hanging in the air, he rose, cried out a promise never forgotten.

The Trailsman they began to call him all across the West: searcher, scout, hunter, the man who could see where others only looked, his skills for hire but not his soul, the man who lived each day to the fullest, yet trailed each tomorrow. Skye Fargo, the Trailsman, the seeker who could take the wildness of a land and the wanting of a woman and make them his own.

1860, near the Wind River Range in the western part of the region that would one day be the state of Wyoming— where renegades roamed freely and settlers bound for the Oregon Territory were easy prey. . . .

1

The big man was almost asleep when he heard the men creeping toward his camp. Skye Fargo's lake-blue eyes snapped open at the soft sound of the first footfall. He listened intently, trying to determine the direction and the distance. Off to the left he saw the Ovaro, standing stock still with its ears pricked. The stallion knew they were about to have visitors too. At his feet the fire crackled while fingers of red and orange flame danced skyward.

Fargo inhaled the crisp night air as he slowly sat up and placed his right hand on the Sharps rifle lying beside him on the blanket. In a holster on his right hip rode a Colt .44. And snug in a sheath in his right boot was his throwing knife. If the visitors turned out to have hostile intentions, they were in for a nasty surprise.

A twig snapped, perhaps forty feet to the east.

Rising into a crouch, Fargo glided to the south until he was out of the fire's glow. He squatted behind a waist-high boulder and scanned the rugged terrain. A full moon provided enough illumination to distinguish details.

He could see the snowcapped peaks of the Wind River range to the northeast. To the south lay level grassland. Off to the west, too far to be seen, was the Wyoming Mountain range he had crossed the day before. He was in a remote, wild region, hundreds of miles from the nearest town. Because of that fact, Fargo was inclined to believe his visitors were Indians. He knew the feared Utes roamed the area he was in, as did occasional bands of aggressive Sioux, Cheyennes, and Arapahos. If a war party from either tribe had spotted his dwindling fire, they would be bound to investigate.

But whoever was out there was making too much noise for Indians. No self-respecting warrior would clump around in the dark as the five or six men were doing who were now converging on the fire from different directions. He heard one coming toward him and hunched low in the shelter of the boulder.

They must be white men, Fargo concluded. If so, what were

they doing in the middle of nowhere? Few whites were willing to brave the elements, possible encounters with wild beasts, and the ever present danger of running into Indians to travel through the uncharted wilderness. There were a number of large ranches many miles to the south, but none in his vicinity.

Fargo heard the soft crunch of boots on the hard soil. He tensed, curled his thumb around the rifle's hammer and his finger around its trigger, and waited for the person to draw nearer. The heavy tread indicated it was a man.

Glancing toward the fire, Fargo spied shadows moving in the night, inky figures stealthily approaching his camp. Then he faced to the east as a man stepped into view beside the boulder. He glimpsed a stocky youth of fifteen or sixteen in a flannel shirt, holding a rifle at the ready. The youth, concentrating on the fire, never looked down.

Fargo let him take two more strides before he stood, stepped behind him, and jabbed the Sharps into the small of the youth's back. "One move and you're dead," he whispered.

The youth halted, frozen in place. "Don't shoot me," he blurted.

There were five other men much closer to the fire. They all had weapons leveled and were gazing around in apparent confusion, frustrated at finding no one there.

Fargo reached around in front of the youth and took the boy's rifle. Then, holding the Sharps in one hand, he prodded the young man forward until they reached the circle of firelight. The night prowlers glanced toward them. "Drop your guns, gentlemen," Fargo declared, staying behind the youth in case they opened fire.

The five shifted, bringing their firearms to bear.

"I won't repeat myself," Fargo advised them. "And if you don't oblige me, this young man will be the first to die."

The tallest of the bunch cursed and tossed his rifle to the ground. "Do as he says," he growled.

The rest promptly complied.

"We don't mean no harm, mister," said the tall one. He had broad shoulders and sported a thick black beard. His clothes were homespun, of the kind typically worn by settlers. "We're not looking for trouble."

"Then you shouldn't go around sneaking up on a man's

camp at midnight," Fargo snapped. "You're just asking for lead in your belly." He nudged the youth with the Sharps. "Walk on over there with your friends."

The young man did so, fearfully looking over his shoulder as if he expected to get a bullet in the back. He halted next to the tall spokesman.

Skye moved closer, a rifle in each hand, the muzzles pointed in the group's general direction. He studied his visitors and noted they were all cast in the settler mold except for a lean hombre on the right.

With the unerring instincts of someone who had spent all of his adult life on the frontier, Fargo rated the lean man as the only dangerous one in the group. The man wore a black frock coat, a white shirt, and a wide-brimmed black hat. His brown hair hung to his shoulders. At his feet lay a fancy Colt Navy with pearl grips. Fargo pegged him as a gambler.

The spokesman appeared rattled by the big man's silence. He licked his lips and said, "If you'll allow me to explain, I'm sure I can clear this misunderstanding up."

"I'm listening," Fargo said, keeping his eyes on the gambler. The man had his arms at his sides in a relaxed posture. He wondered if there might be a derringer hidden up one of the man's sleeves. Gamblers were notorious for such a tactic.

"My name is Seth Purdy," the spokesman said, and nodded at the youth. "This is my son, Adam. All of us here are with a wagon train. We're on our way to Oregon."

"Oregon?" Fargo repeated in surprise. South of where they stood, perhaps twenty-five or thirty miles as the crow flew, lay the Oregon Trail, the rutted ribbon of well-traveled earth that wound from Independence, Missouri, to the Oregon Territory. Thousands of settlers in their big wagons had arleady traveled its course, and hundreds more did so every month during the spring and summer. "What are you doing so far north?"

"Chasing the band of cutthroats who attacked our wagons yesterday morning," Seth stated.

"You're chasing Indians?" Fargo asked, finding the notion comical. Purdy's group stood as much chance of overtaking a raiding party as a turtle did of catching a jackrabbit.

The man in the wide-brimmed hat answered. "Not Indians," he said softly. "The wagon train was hit by Blue Raven and his men."

Fargo frowned. Blue Raven was an infamous half-breed, born of a Sioux father and a white mother, who had been butchering whites for over six years. His band, rumored to consist of twelve to fifteen hardened killers, roamed the fringes of Indian country and conducted lightning attacks on small settlements and isolated ranches and farms whenever the mood struck them. The army, despite its best efforts, had been unable to put an end to the attacks. "How do you know it was Blue Raven?" he asked.

"The leader of the band fit Blue Raven's description," the gambler said. "He was wearing a dark beaver hat, an old army coat, and a red scarf."

The description certainly fit that of the renowned renegade, Fargo reflected. Blue Raven had obtained the beaver hat, so the story went, from a trapper he'd scalped. The coat came from a soldier who had been part of a patrol ambushed and wiped out near the Medicine Bow River. And the scarf reportedly once belonged to some poor soul who had been with a small wagon train attacked several years ago. Every man, woman, and child had been slain and horribly mutilated.

"We weren't expecting much trouble from hostiles," Purdy said. "We had forty-two wagons and plenty and able fighting men."

"What happened?" Fargo asked.

Purdy scowled. "They hit us at dawn and tried to steal our horses, but some of the animals became skittish. A sentry saw Blue Raven and his men and gave the alarm. He was shot dead on the spot."

"I saw it happen," the youth spoke up. "The sentry was shot to pieces."

"We spilled out of our wagons," Purdy went on. "Three more men were shot before we even realized what was happening. By the time we got organized and began to fight back, Blue Raven's men had taken a third of our stock." He paused, lowering his voice. "And that's not all."

"What do you mean?" Fargo inquired.

"Somehow, in all of the confusion, those bastards

took a twenty-two-year-old woman," Purdy revealed.

Now Fargo understood the reason the group was so set on catching the renegade. And he didn't blame them. The woman's life would mean nothing to Blue Raven; he'd as soon slit her throat as look at her. "This woman have a name?"

"Susan Chambers. Her pa took a bullet trying to save her and now he'll be laid up for over a month," Purdy said. "We rode out about two hours after the attack. We've been on Blue Raven's trail ever since."

"He came this way?" Fargo asked. Since war parties were frequently abroad in the region, he'd been extra alert the past few days. Yet he hadn't seen any sign of the band of renegades.

"We think so," Seth replied. "To tell you the truth, none of us are much good at tracking. We're farmers and clerks and such." He nodded at the man in the wide-brimmed hat. "All except Calhoun, here. He makes his living at cards."

Fargo regarded the gambler with interest. So his hunch had been right. But what was a man like Calhoun doing with a bunch of nesters?

"We lost the tracks early today," Purdy disclosed. "Since then we've been wandering in circles trying to pick up the trail again. We can't give up until we rescue Susan."

Seth Purdy nodded. "Now you know our story. Mind if I ask who you might be?"

"Skye Fargo."

Calhoun cocked his head to one side. "Aren't you the one they call the Trailsman?"

"Some folks call me that," Fargo admitted. He let the rifle barrels droop and walked around the fire to hand Adam's weapon back. "Here. The next time, remember it helps to have eyes in the back of your head."

The youth grinned nervously. "Thanks. I will."

"Skye Fargo," Seth said slowly, his brow knitting in thought. "I've heard of you. They say you're one of the best scouts who ever lived."

"I get around," Fargo said, moving over to his bedroll. He leaned down and propped the Sharps on his saddle, knowing what was coming and pondering whether to agree or not.

"Will you help us find the girl?" Seth requested. "With

your help we stand a chance. Otherwise, you know what will happen to her.''

The Trailsman straightened. Yes, he did know. If Blue Raven let her live, she'd be abused by every man in the band or sold, perhaps to the Sioux or the Cheyenne. If she was strong, she might cope and survive. But she would be scarred for life where it counted the most, in the depths of her soul. He'd seen such tormented souls before and disliked the idea of it happening to a young woman fresh from the East.

"Please," Purdy said. "I know you have your own affairs to tend to and what I'm asking is a terrible imposition, but surely you can spare a day or two to help us look? If we don't find her by then, we might as well give it up anyway.''

Fargo mulled his decision. There was no reason why he couldn't lend a hand. He was on his way to the Nebraska Territory to visit a lady friend whose charms would help him relax after weeks in the wilderness. A delay of a few days wouldn't matter one way or the other. "I reckon I can help you," he said.

Seth Purdy beamed and several of the other men voiced their gratitude. "Mind if we pick up our guns now?" Seth inquired.

"Go right ahead," Fargo said and squatted by his saddle-bags. "Would any of you care for some coffee?"

"Would we!" young Adam declared. "We've hardly had a bite to eat and nothing but water to drink since we left the wagon train.''

Fargo unfastened one of the flaps and reached inside. Suddenly he heard the Ovaro whinny. Shifting, he saw the pinto gazing to the north, its nostrils flaring as it tested the breeze for scent. He'd learned long ago to trust that horse; it didn't spook easily and always let him know when something, or someone, was nearby.

Calhoun was sliding his Colt into its holster. He glanced at the stallion, then at the Trailsman. "Is something wrong?" he asked.

"We may have company," Fargo announced, standing and stepping away from the fire to minimize the target he presented should there be Indians or worse out there. The Ovaro continued to sniff and peer northward. It could be a mountain lion or a bear, he reasoned. Either would likely give the fire a wide berth.

Seth Purdy and the others were looking anxiously in all directions. "What kind of company?" he wanted to know.

"I don't know yet," Fargo said. "But I wouldn't stand there in the open if I was you."

Startled, Seth motioned for the others to move into the shadows. Even as he did, the loud drumming of pounding hooves filled the night.

Large forms materialized in the darkness, sweeping toward the camp in a ragged line. Fargo counted at least seven mounted men. Loud, fierce whoops issued from their throats and gunfire blossomed. He bent low and angled to the left, drawing the .44.

One of the settlers screeched and fell, his hands clutching his throat.

The incoming riders swerved the east well clear of the camp, blasting away all the while.

Fargo abruptly realized the Ovaro was in the line of fire. He ran to the stallion, snapping off two shots at the vague galloping shapes. Since the bridle was beside the saddle, he would have to make do without it. Vaulting onto the pinto's back, he seized its mane and wheeled the animal to the south. Bullets whizzed through the air, sounding like angry hornets in flight.

He goaded the stallion forward and hunched low, twisting so he could aim at the circling figures and snap off another shot. Calhoun and the settlers were returning fire, but except for the gambler, they were shooting recklessly.

Skye couldn't understand why the attackers were swinging around the camp instead of charging straight through. For that matter, why hadn't they simply sprung an ambush from the dark instead of attacking on horseback? The next instant he had an answer when Seth Purdy bellowed angrily, "Our horses! They're going after our horses!"

Fargo cut to the left, realizing the settlers' mounts must be to the east. He cocked the Colt and rode after the attackers, listening to them yell as they drove the settlers' animals off. A horse and rider materialized ahead. The man had halted, and Fargo detected the dull glint of metal as a revolver was aimed directly at him.

2

Instinctively, Fargo squeezed off a shot of his own and saw the man pitch from the saddle. He closed on his fallen foe, who was trying to rise, the revolver still grasped in an unsteady hand. At a range of less than three yards Fargo sent a bullet into the man's brain. Then he was past the body and pulling on the Ovaro's mane to stop the big horse, trying to orient himself and determine the location of the attackers.

The firing had almost stopped. One or two of the settlers were foolishly wasting ammunition. The attackers were racing to the northeast, no longer visible, their passage marked by their triumphant shouts and the thundering of their horses.

Fargo wasn't about to go after them, not without the Sharps and the rest of his gear. He turned the pinto and stopped beside the man he'd slain. Sliding down, he crouched to examine the body.

Bronzed, weathered features that bore evidence of white and Indian ancestry were contorted in a death grimace. Clearly a half-breed, the man wore buckskins that had seen better days. An ebony stain on his chest and a hole in his forehead marked where Fargo's shots had scored.

"Fargo? Where are you?"

The Trailsman turned at the shout to see Seth Purdy, his son, and Calhoun slowly advancing in his general direction. "Over here," he answered and stood. By now even the sound of the attackers' animals had faded and a disquieting stillness shrouded the moon-bathed landscape.

"You nailed one of the bastards!" Seth exclaimed delightedly as he ran up. "I don't think I hit one."

"Me either," Adam said.

Calhoun stared at the corpse and began reloading his Colt. "Unless I miss my guess, that's one of the half-breeds who was riding with Blue Raven."

"Likely so," Fargo agreed. He began replacing the spent cartridges in his .44. "About half the band paid us a visit."

Seth leaned over the renegade. "How did they know we were here?"

"Blue Raven hasn't survived all these years by being a nitwit," Fargo said. "He probably sent some of his men to check their backtrail. They saw you and figured they'd bide their time and hit you when you least expected it."

"But all they did was take our horses," Adam said.

"Out here that's enough," Fargo commented, dismayed at how green these men were. "A man on foot doesn't stand much of a chance unless he knows how to live off the land like an Indian. And without your horses you can't trail Blue Raven. Those men knew exactly what they were doing."

"What will we do?" Adam asked apprehensively.

"I'm not about to do anything until morning," Fargo said. "Then I'll follow their tracks and try to recover your animals. If I can't, we'll try something else." Placing a hand on his stallion's neck, he guided the Ovaro toward the fire. Two of the pilgrims were sprawled on the ground, both motionless. The last survivor stood between them, gawking in horrified disbelief.

These men were like fish out of water, Fargo reflected. They had no business trailing Blue Raven. If they continued, they'd undoubtedly wind up being slaughtered. He figured the wisest thing to do would be to take them to the wagon train and light out after the young woman himself. But first they needed horses.

The gambler and the Purdys returned to the fire. Calhoun wore a thoughtful expression and kept glancing at Fargo.

"We'll bury your friends," Skye proposed. "Then we'll put out the fire and catch some sleep. I want to leave at first light."

"Sleep?" Seth said, as if the idea was preposterous. "I don't think I could after what just happened. Shouldn't we post guards until daylight?"

"If it will make you feel better, do it," Fargo said. "But Blue Raven's men aren't about to come back. They know that you're no threat to them now. They plan to put as much distance as they can between the wagon train and them."

"How can you be sure?" Seth inquired.

"I'm just putting myself in their shoes. They'd expect you

to send riders to Fort Laramie to report the attack," Fargo said, and paused. "You did, didn't you?"

Seth nodded. "Four of our men rode out right after the attack. They should be a third of the way there by now. With any luck, an army patrol will reach the wagons in nine or ten days."

"And Blue Raven can be halfway to Canada by then," Fargo noted. He didn't bother to add that the army would never catch the wily renegade. The girl's fate was as good as sealed unless he could rescue her.

"I don't like the notion of being stranded here," young Adam declared and cast a wistful gaze to the northeast. "Not when Susan is in their dirty hands."

The youth's melancholy made Fargo realize that Adam Purdy cared a great deal for Susan Chambers. He wondered if there might be something between them. Perhaps Adam was older than he'd imagined, or maybe it was a simple case of infatuation. Whatever, it mattered little to him. "We should bury the dead right away," he remarked. "The scent of the blood might attract predators."

"I'll see if we can find some branches or stones to dig with," Seth volunteered and moved off searching the ground. His son and the other survivors trailed along.

Not so Calhoun. He stared at the Trailsman for a moment, then said quietly so the others wouldn't hear, "You know as well as I do that they don't stand a prayer of saving that woman. If you get our horses back, you should tell them to give up and rejoin the wagon train."

Fargo studied the gambler's angular features. "Why did you tag along if you know they're wasting their time?"

Calhoun patted his Colt. "I'm a fair hand with this. I figured I could keep them out of trouble."

"Do you know the Chambers woman?" Fargo asked.

"Not personally. I've seen her on the train, but we never spoke," Calhoun said. He turned and gazed into the distance. "None of the settlers were partial to my company."

Fargo could easily imagine why. Professional gamblers were lone wolves who tended to associate with their own kind and were invariably shunned by so-called decent folks. It was odd that a man like Calhoun was with the train. The

Oregon Territory might be ripe with opportunities for farmers, lumberjacks, trappers, and such, but the gaming prospects were limited in comparison to the big money to be made in wild-and-woolly cities like Denver and Kansas City. Those who made their living bucking the odds at poker, faro, and keno tables ordinarily flocked to where the gambling action was heaviest.

Skye wondered why Calhoun was turning his back on all of that. There were some mining camps and boomtowns out Oregon way where the gambler would probably make a fair living, but nothing to compare with the pickings in the Rockies. Why, Denver alone was a literal gold mine, thanks to the discovery of the precious metal in that area just two years before. But he wasn't about to pry into the man's personal affairs.

Someone abruptly came running toward them and they turned.

"Mr. Fargo. Mr. Calhoun. Look at what we found," declared Adam Purdy, racing up with an extra rifle held in his left hand. He stepped close to the fire so they could see the weapon clearly. "My pa found this. It's got blood on it."

Fargo took the rifle and found a sticky blotch on the stock and the trigger guard. One of Blue Raven's men must have been hit and dropped it, he deduced. Good. A wounded man would slow the renegades down.

"Pa wanted me to give it to you," Adam said, pivoting. "I've got to go help him." He dashed into the darkness.

Moving to his blanket, Fargo sat down and deposited the rifle beside it. He thought of something he'd neglected to ask and looked at the gambler. "Is Seth Purdy the wagon boss of your train?"

"No. A man named Miller is. He's one of the ones who lit out for Fort Laramie."

"Did he leave Purdy in charge?"

Calhoun shook his head. "A fellow called Webber is handling that chore."

"So Purdy just took off after Blue Raven on his own?" Fargo inquired.

"Yeah. He asked for volunteers and only a few spoke up.

Most of the other men didn't want to leave their wives and families alone," Calhoun said. "Why?"

"Just wondered," Fargo responded. It increased his estimation of Seth Purdy to know the man was simply being a Good Samaritan. The best of intentions, however, never prevented anyone from getting a bullet in the brain. He leaned back and gazed idly at the writhing flames.

Soon the Purdys and their companion returned bearing broken branches and long, slender stones.

"We're all set to dig," Seth announced, looking at Skye. He motioned at the other man. "Before I forget, this here is Ed Flanders."

Fargo nodded at the settler and went to rise.

"Don't bother," Seth said. "We'll handle the burying. These are our friends. There's no need for you to help."

"Suit yourself," Fargo said. There was no reason to dispute the point. "But take the bodies out at least twenty-five yards. I'll have some coffee ready by the time you get back."

"Thanks," Seth said. He gave his rifle and branch to his son, then leaned down hooking his hands under the arms of a dead man and started to haul the heavy corpse to the west.

Fargo noticed that Calhoun made no effort to help. The gambler cupped his hands behind his back and took to slowly pacing back and forth, his chin lowered, his brow knit in thought. Fargo got the impression Calhoun was worried about something. He busied himself preparing coffee and had the last of his meager supply brewing in a small tin pot by the time the weary settlers were done planting the stiffening bodies of their two dead friends and the fallen half-breed.

"Whew! That was hard work," Seth commented as he walked into the firelight. "The ground hereabouts is like iron."

Adam seemed disturbed and withdrawn. He took a seat and morosely stared into space.

The man named Flanders gazed at Fargo. "Do you really think you can track those vermin and recover our horses?"

"I'll try my best," Fargo proposed.

"And if he can't do it, no one can," Calhoun threw in.

Mildly surprised at the compliment, Fargo sat back and

sipped at his cup. He'd have to share it with the others, but he didn't mind. Being hospitable to strangers was a fact of life in the West. He knew that back East things were different; the people in places like New York City and Philadelphia were too caught up in their own lives to give someone they didn't know the time of day. Although a loner by nature, he much preferred the friendlier folks in the West to those who always walked around with their noses in the air. Give him the vast outdoors, the uncharted expanse between the Mississippi River and the Pacific Ocean, and decent people any day.

Off in the distance a coyote howled.

Adam started. "Do you think that was an Indian?"

"It was the real article," Fargo assured him.

"How can you tell the difference?" Adam asked.

"Because as good as Indians are at imitating animal sounds, there isn't a warrior alive who can yip exactly like a coyote. If you'd heard as many of the critters as I have, you'd be able to tell which was which," Fargo said. He took another sip and passed the cup to Seth, then settled down on his blanket and laced his fingers behind his head.

"Do you have any idea where the nearest water is?" Seth inquired. "Without our canteens, we're apt to become a bit thirsty by tomorrow afternoon."

"It will be hot tomorrow," Fargo conceded. "I'll be on the lookout for a stream when I go after your horses."

"We'll be forever in your debt," Seth said. "I don't know how we can ever repay you."

"There's no need," Fargo said.

"Just make sure Blue Raven doesn't get his hands on you," Calhoun mentioned. "If you don't make it back here, we might windup digging our own graves."

Fargo closed his eyes and said nothing. He knew the truth when he heard it.

A resplendent red-and-yellow halo rimmed the eastern horizon when Fargo finished saddling the pinto and swung up. The Sharps rested loosely in its saddle case, ready for action. He gripped the reins and glanced at the settlers. They were all sound asleep, too worn-out by their strenuous ordeal to stay up all night despite their concern about being attacked again. Only Calhoun was awake, sitting hunched over by the fire. He looked up and gave a curt nod.

Fargo did likewise and pointed the Ovaro to the northeast. He yawned and shook his head to dispel lingering tendrils of sleep clouding his mind. He'd need all of his wits about him if he hoped to recover the stolen animals, and they were his first order of business simply because he figured the renegades responsible for taking them were much closer than Blue Raven and the rest of the band.

He found the trail with no difficulty. Twelve horses left enough tracks for a six-year-old to follow. It was easy to distinguish the settlers' mounts from those of the renegades since shod hooves made distinctly deeper tracks than those that weren't. Not more than fifteen minutes after leaving camp the trail angled sharply to the north.

The sun rose above the rim of the earth, gradually warming the air. Abundant wildlife was everywhere. Twice, Fargo saw hawks and once, a majestic eagle soared far overhead. A herd of alert pronghorn antelope regarded him warily, then bounded off in great, graceful twenty-foot leaps. Able to run faster than any horse that ever lived, the pronghorns were soon out of sight.

Throughout the morning the Ovaro spooked jackrabbits, ground squirrels, and prairie dogs. Once, off to the west, Fargo spied several grazing elk. They continued to eat, unruffled by his presence.

Fargo recognized a few of the prominent peaks lining the Wind River range, peaks well-known to every Indian and frontiersman who frequently traveled through the region. Fremont Peak and Lizard Head Peak, in particular, were readily identified and enabled him to mark his location throughout the morning hours.

It became apparent early on that the renegades were making for the remote area bordering the Wind River range to the northwest. Consisting of a series of verdant, well-watered valleys winding among steep mountains, it was an ideal area in which to hide.

Fargo did not come across any streams, but he guessed that he must be close to the Green River, which flowed in a serpentine course from north to south. He turned out to be right. When the sun was an hour shy of midday, he came to the top of a low rise and there, shimmering and inviting, lay the river to his west. He had paralleled it all morning without realizing how close it truly was.

He noticed the tracks led toward the river. There was no sign of the renegades or the stolen horses and he assumed they were long gone. Intending to quench the Ovaro's thirst, he rode toward a stand of trees on the east bank. The temperature had climbed into the low eighties already and promised to peak in the nineties.

Thinking of how nice it would be to splash cool water on his face, Fargo let himself become distracted. The price of his neglect became apparent when he detected movement in the trees a fraction of a second before a rifle boomed.

3

The shot missed Fargo's right cheek by inches. He instantly brought the stallion to a gallop and drew the Colt, heading for the north side of the stand, knowing he would be picked off if he tried to get back over the rise. A puff of gun smoke marked the spot where the rifleman was concealed in the dense foliage. Anticipating a second shot close on the heels of the first, Fargo swerved the Ovaro from side to side. Surprisingly, he covered thirty yards before the next shot blasted.

Again the hidden ambusher missed, but not by much. Fargo concluded there was only one man, which evened the odds. He took hasty aim at the second cloud of gun smoke and fired, doubting he would hit a thing but hoping he would force the man to duck low and buy him time to reach the trees.

The third and final shot cracked just as the stallion plunged into the vegetation. A slug smacked into a tree trunk near Fargo's right elbow. He didn't stop until he was behind a thicket, and then he reined up so hard the Ovaro skidded to a halt with dirt and grass flying out from under its hooves.

Vaulting to the ground, Skye holstered the .44 and whipped the Sharps out. Crouching, he dashed into the undergrowth and paused behind a trunk to look and listen. Not so much as a sparrow stirred. He cautiously moved toward the gunman, using whatever cover presented itself, blending into the background as an Indian would.

He was easing to his elbows and knees to crawl behind a large log when he heard a cough and its wheezing aftermath. Removing his hat, he snaked halfway along the log and carefully elevated his head above the top. More coughing erupted, punctuated by a gurgling whine.

Had he hit the rifleman? The odds of so lucky a shot were sky-high. Then another explanation occurred to him. Maybe it was the renegade wounded during the attack last night. If so, why was he all by his lonesome?

Bushes moved, and a buckskin clad form materialized, heading for the river.

Fargo realized it was a young Sioux. The warrior held an old flintlock, one of the inferior trade guns frequently received from greedy fur company representatives in exchange for prime pelts. No wonder the man had only been able to fire three times. In light of the bloodstain extending from the warrior's left shoulder to his knee, that accomplishment was remarkable.

Slowly raising the Sharps, he supported the barrel on the log and took a bead on the warrior. If he could, he wanted the buck alive to answer a few questions. "Drop your gun!" he bellowed.

The warrior whirled, his wide eyes frantically scouring the vegetation for the source of the voice, and tried to level the flintlock.

Taking a breath to steady the rifle, Fargo aimed at the brave's right shoulder and fired. The impact lifted the warrior from his feet and hurled him into a pine tree, the flintlock clattering to the earth. Shoving upright, Fargo palmed the Colt and raced over to the prone brave.

His eyes still open, his lips quivering, the Sioux now had a hole on his right side that complemented the smaller hole on his left. He focused on the big man standing over him. Fueled by hostility, his features transformed into a mask of hate. "White dog," he snapped harshly in heavily accented English. He attempted to rise, but couldn't.

"You're one of Blue Raven's band," Fargo observed, lowering the .44. The brave posed no danger, not with the copious amount of blood pumping from the new wound. Combined with the blood the warrior had previously lost, Fargo guessed the man was close to being bled dry.

The Sioux bobbed his chin once. "He will take your hair, white pig."

"Where is he?"

"I tell you nothing."

Even on the threshold of death, the warrior radiated defiance. Fargo had heard that all of Blue Raven's men hated whites; that was the single common bond that kept such a volatile group of killers together. Just as there were white bigots who despised Indians simply because the hue of their skin was different, so there were Indians and half-breeds who detested whites for the same flimsy reason.

Again the brave struggled to stand. Far too weak, he sank down and scowled at his own impotence.

"Why did your friends leave you behind?" Fargo inquired, hoping a change of subject would get the Sioux to talk.

The warrior glowered and said nothing.

"I reckon there's no loyalty among yellow-bellies," Fargo remarked with deliberate disdain. "Cowards who murder innocent people and steal young women aren't the kind to stick together in a pinch."

Simmering anger caused the brave's face to become scarlet. He tried to speak but only sputtered. The blood from his wound flowed faster.

"Yep. They must have figured you were too much of a liability and left you to die," Fargo said.

"I wanted to stay!" the Sioux declared with fiery passion. "I did not want to slow them down."

"So when they broke camp this morning, you stayed here."

"We never made camp," the brave asserted. "This was as far as I could go."

Fargo had learned something important. If the renegades had ridden all night and were still pushing to catch up with Blue Raven, overtaking them any time soon would be impossible. Maybe in another twenty-four hours, if he was lucky, he'd find them. Then it would take another, possibly a day and a half, to retrace his route, since the stolen mounts were bound to be tired. In the meantime, the Purdys, Calhoun and Flanders would be at the mercy of the elements and without food and water.

As much as Fargo wanted to go after Susan Chambers, he couldn't very well leave the four men to fend for themselves since none of them possessed wilderness survival skills. Stranded without horses and water, they might well perish. He had to make certain they were safe before he took off after Blue Raven, who would already have had a two-and-a-half day lead.

The brave coughed and feebly moved his arms. "Kill me, white dog."

"Why should I waste the bullet?" Fargo retorted. "You're at death's door anyway."

Grimacing in pain, the warrior spoke in a hoarse whisper, "Finish me off, bastard. It is all I ask."

"I don't do favors for folks who try to kill me," Fargo said. He tucked the Sharps under his left arm, picked up the flintlock in his left hand, and started to walk off.

"Damn you!" the Sioux snarled. "You would finish off a lame horse. Do the same for me."

Skye paused and glanced over his shoulder. "I happen to hold horses in higher regard than murderring sons of bitches like you." He took another step, then halted, struck by a thought. "Maybe I will oblige you. But I expect something in return first."

The brave's features adopted a quizzical cast. "What?" he rasped.

"Blue Raven took a woman from the wagon train your band attacked," Fargo said. "Is she still with him? What does he have planned for her?"

"Go to your white Hell, white man. My lips are sealed."

"Then lie there and rot," Fargo said and moved toward the log. He took only four strides when the warrior called out weakly.

"Stop. I will tell you."

Fargo turned. Agony lined the Sioux's face and the man was trembling. "I'm listening."

It was a full fifteen seconds before the warrior spoke, and he did so only with supreme effort. "The woman is alive. She has not been harmed."

"Has anyone abused her?"

"Not that I know. I think Blue Raven will sell her for a good price. Maybe not. Maybe he will keep her for himself. He likes her hair," the brave said and went limp in exhaustion.

"What about her hair?" Fargo asked.

The warrior inhaled loudly. "It is the color of the sun. Very lovely." He abruptly convulsed, his limbs thrashing.

When the fit subsided, he tilted his head and stared at the muscular man in buckskins. "Do it."

"I reckon you've earned it," Fargo said, lifting the Colt. He took careful aim on the bridge of the brave's nose, cocked the hammer until it clicked, then stroked the trigger. The slug cored the Sioux's forehead and the man arched his spine, then expelled all the air in his lungs in a last, lingering breath. Fargo slid the Colt into its holster and went to get his hat. He hastened thoughtfully to the thicket where the stallion was hidden.

For the time being at least, the Chambers woman appeared to be safe. As safe as she could be under the circumstances. Since her four would-be rescuers were at the greater risk, it was all the confirmation he needed that he'd made the right decision in deciding to aid them first. Not that he particularly liked the idea of leaving her in Blue Raven's clutches.

He reached the pinto and tied the flintlock between the cantle and his bedroll. After sliding the Sharps into its case, he forked leather and rode to the east bank of the shallow Green River. The Ovaro drank greedily and wasn't inclined to stop when he finally pulled it away from the cool water. He took but a few moments to dismount, splash the refreshing liquid on his face, and sip a handful. Then he was in the saddle again and riding hard to the south, staying close to the river this time. The hours dragged by until he reached a point approximately due west of his camp.

Fargo swung eastward, scouring the terrain for the quartet. The blazing sun hung just above the western horizon and he wanted to locate them before nightfall. If he came up on them after dark, they just might be foolhardy or spooked enough to shoot first and identify him later. He'd have to call out once he saw their campfire.

But he saw no trace of smoke. In due course he reached the general area where he was certain his camp had been. He reined up, rose in the stirrups, and surveyed the land. A vaguely familiar boulder on his right drew him in that direction. A minute later he sat three yards from the blackened embers of the fire he had made the night before.

The four men were gone.

Fargo's first thought was that Indians had found them. He

dropped down to minutely examine the ground. The earth bore no evidence of a struggle. Bending over the charred embers, he touched them with the tips of his fingers. They were cold, indicating the fire had been out since at least noon, probably earlier. Making a circuit of the campsite, he found where the four men had walked off, heading to the southeast.

What the hell were they up to?

He climbed on the stallion and rode on their trail, annoyed by the unexpected development. Had they been there, he was going to lead them to the Green River, then head for the wagon train to obtain horses. Now he would waste a great deal of time tracking the fools down.

The sun dipped ever lower.

Fargo hoped the men had only traveled a short distance, but as the Ovaro's shadow lengthened to mammoth proportions he realized he wouldn't catch them before the sun set. The whole time, in the back of his mind he fretted about the fate of the Chambers woman. It would serve the four lunkheads right if he simply abandoned them and went after her.

Evening settled in and gradually gave way to the ghostly gloom of night. A gorgeous full moon rose in the east, causing the snow that topped the Wind River range to glisten in the feeble light. A cool breeze from the northwest fanned the high grass.

Following the tracks from horseback became impossible. Fargo continued in the direction they had been heading, hoping the four men hadn't deviated from their course. A small hill reared ahead.

From the other side came a single shot.

Fargo spurred the Ovaro into a canter. He went straight up the hill and halted just below the crest to avoid affording a silhouette to potentially hostile eyes. Cheerful whoops greeted his ears and he distinguished four figures clustered around a shoulder-high mound close to the bottom of the slope. Cupping a hand to his mouth, he shouted, "Purdy? Calhoun?"

"Fargo?" came in immediate, delightful reply from Seth Purdy. "Come see what we've bagged."

Over the rim Skye went, putting a lid on his temper as

he rode down to them. The mound turned out to be a dead buffalo. Seth Purdy, Adam, and Flanders were laughing happily and admiring the dead beast while Calhoun stood moodily to one side.

The gambler looked up as the frontiersman stopped, his mouth creased in a sarcastic smile. "Glad you found us before we wound up in Missouri."

"Leaving the camp wasn't your idea, I take it?" Fargo inquired, his steely eyes on Seth Purdy.

"We'd still be there if it had been up to me," Calhoun replied testily, his gaze on the same person.

Adam twisted and motioned at the buffalo. "Ain't this terrific, Mṛ. Fargo? We'll have prime meat for dinner, all we can eat."

Saying nothing, Fargo eased to the ground. Seth and Flanders were hardly paying any attention to him; they were too elated over the kill. He walked up to Seth, spun the hayseed around and gripped the front of the startled man's shirt. "Were you born a jackass or have you just naturally become one over the years?"

"What?" Seth blurted. "What did I do?"

Fargo gave the man a shove in disgust. "I told you to stay put until I got back, remember?"

"But we were hungry and thirsty," Seth protested. "We figured we would do a little hunting and search for water at the same time. But all the game we saw lit out before we could get a good shot." He nodded proudly at the buffalo. "Until now, that is."

"I shot it," Flanders spoke up, grinning like a ten-year-old who had killed his first pheasant. "The dumb thing just stood there and let me kill it."

Fargo stepped closer to the buffalo, a female in her prime. He noticed a prominent bulge on her exposed side and moved around to study her belly. "No wonder she just stood there," he said in disgust. "She was about to drop her calf."

Flanders tried to swallow air and held his rifle out as if it had suddenly become distasteful. "I didn't know."

"What difference does it make?" Seth Purdy asked. "Food is food, I say. Out here a man survives any way he can. Let's butcher this critter and fill our bellies."

"But Pa—" Adam said uncertainly.

Seth spun on his son. "But what? You were the hungriest of us all, as I recall. Well, I promised we'd find something to eat and we did. Butchering this buffalo is no different from butchering a cow, for crying out loud."

"But we never butchered a pregnant cow," Adam said.

"It's not like you raised this buffalo from a calf," Seth stated angrily. "It's no better than a deer or an antelope." He looked at the carcass. "So let's get to work. I can taste the succulent meat already."

Fargo found himself disliking Seth Purdy immensely. His opinion of the man had done a complete reversal. He turned and climbed onto the Ovaro.

"Where are you going, Mr. Fargo?" Adam inquired anxiously.

"To your wagon train to get some horses," Skye informed him. He pointed westward. "At dawn head out and go about four miles. You'll reach the Green River. If you're there when I return, you can ride back to your train. If you're not, don't expect me to come looking for you."

"Wait a minute," Seth said. "Do you mean you didn't have any luck getting our animals back from those renegades?"

"Now you ask," Fargo said dryly. "No, I didn't. I did learn the Chambers woman will be safe for the time being. No thanks to you."

"I don't understand what's eating you," Seth said.

Fargo leaned forward, his voice brittle as he snapped, "Do you have any notion of how much time you've made me waste traipsing over the countryside trying to find you? If I reach Susan Chambers too late to save her, you'll be partly to blame." He saw his words take effect and sighed. "Now where exactly are these wagons of yours?"

"Do you know where Absaroka Ridge is?" Calhoun answered.

Fargo nodded.

"The wagons are camped along the creek bordering the ridge to the east," Calhoun disclosed.

"You can expect to see me before noon tomorrow if all goes well," Fargo informed them. He saw the boy gazing at him with a fainthearted expression and gave him a reassuring grin. Then he wheeled the Ovaro and rode to the southwest.

If not for Calhoun and Adam, Fargo reflected, he'd pursue Blue Raven right then and there. Even with the delay, though, locating the renegades shouldn't prove too difficult. They would stick to the waterways, going from river to stream to spring or wherever else water was available. The task would be time consuming, but eventually he would rescue Susan Chambers.

Eventually. The word seared into his conscience like a red-hot knife. What if he'd made the wrong decision? He'd weighed the four lives of the men afoot in hostile Indian country against her single life and concluded that saving four was more important. But if things went wrong, he knew with a dreadful certainty that he'd never be able to look at himself in a mirror again.

4

The stallion performed superbly. After crossing the Green River the lay of the land was essentially flat, enabling Fargo to push the pinto much faster than he would when traveling over mountainous terrain at night. His main worry was having one of the Ovaro's hooves become caught in a prairie dog hole or some other animal burrow, but fate smiled on him. The hours passed rapidly. Dawn was still several hours off when he saw flickering pinpoints of light to the southwest, pinpoints that rapidly grew in size to become nine or ten campfires. Since they were located near Absaroka Ridge, they must belong to the settlers.

Fargo galloped toward them. In their combined glow he spied dozens of wagons and the shimmering surface of the creek beyond them. There were plenty of trees dotting the area that would afford shade during the heat of the day. Whoever had picked the site had done well. He saw forms moving near a fire at the center of the camp and made toward it.

Without warning two men carrying rifles materialized out of the night and trained their weapons on him. "Hold up!" one bellowed.

To disobey would prompt them to open fire. Fargo brought the weary stallion to a halt in front of the pair and nipped their anticipated questions in the bud by declaring, "Take me to Webber, pronto."

The men stared at him, clearly puzzled, apparently uncertain if they should trust him or not. Neither made a move to lower his rifle.

"Are you hard of hearing?" Fargo asked. "I'm here to get mounts for Seth Purdy and I need to see Webber right away."

"Purdy, did you say?" one of the sentries responded. "Follow me, mister. We'll rouse Tom out of the sack for you."

Patting the Ovaro for a job well done, Fargo let the men

lead him to a fire where three settlers were seated. All three stood at his approach.

"Get Webber," the one sentry stated. "Hurry."

A portly man ran off.

Dismounting, Fargo stretched, heedless of the inquisitive gazes fixed on him. His body ached and he wished he could catch some sleep, but he was determined to stay awake until he reached the Green River. He gazed at the stallion and realized it was tuckered out after spending all day and most of the night on the go. If he wanted to make good time returning to Calhoun and Purdy, he had to let the horse rest for an hour or two.

There was a commotion at a nearby wagon. The portly man came back with a tall pilgrim in tow. This newcomer wore pants and his undershirt, nothing more. "I'm Tom Webber," he announced. "I hear you want to see me."

"Skye Fargo," Fargo said, offering his hand. As he shook he heard whispered comments from several of the others. They knew of him. "Seth Purdy had his horses stolen by some of Blue Raven's bunch. If you'll get four animals ready to go, I'll ride out as soon as my pinto is rested."

Webber digested the news somberly. "Four horses?" he said. "There are six men with Seth."

"There *were* six," Fargo stated. "His son, Flanders, and Calhoun are all that's left of the rescue party. They're waiting for me about thirty miles north of here."

The portly man took a half-step forward. "What about Susan Chambers, mister? Did they find her?"

"No," Fargo replied. "She's still Blue Raven's captive. I aim to go after her myself as soon as I deliver these horses."

"Someone go tell her father," Webber directed and after a man ran toward the wagons to the south, he gestured at the fire. "You look like you could use a rest yourself. How about some coffee? I'd like to hear everything that's happened."

"First I need my horse tended to," Fargo said. "Plenty of feed and water, if you have it."

"Hell, we'll give it a rubdown, too," Webber offered, and glanced at a sentry. "Davis, the job is yours. And get our four best horses saddled."

"They'll be ready to go when Fargo is," Davis promised, departing.

Fargo gratefully sat near the fire. Someone shoved a cup of steaming coffee at him and he gulped it, feeling an invigorating burning sensation all the way down to his stomach. He had to admit that he was as tired as the Ovaro and could use a break himself.

"How did you happen to run into Purdy?" Webber inquired.

In brief detail Fargo related the sequence of events and concluded with, "So you can see why it's important for me to ride out as soon as I can."

From his rear came a musical female voice. "I hope you have the time to say hello to an old friend."

Rising, Fargo turned to discover a buxom redhead in an ankle-length gray dress, a red shawl draped over her slender shoulders. She walked up to him, grinning in a carefree fashion, her green eyes twinkling in the firelight.

"Don't tell me that you've forgotten me so soon, Skye," she said.

It took a second for Fargo to place her. And then vivid memories of the two wild weeks he spent in St. Louis a half-dozen summers ago filled his head, and he smiled wryly. "Gretchen Carpenter," he said softly, thinking of the last time he'd seen her. He'd been on his way out the door of their room at the Fairmont Hotel, and she had blown him a kiss from a rumpled bed they had used strenuously for the better part of three days.

"It's Gretchen Rice now," she replied, stepping forward and giving him a friendly and ever-so-proper hug.

"Where's the lucky man?" Fargo asked. "I'd like to meet him." Out of the corner of his eye he noticed Webber flinch, as if he'd asked a question he shouldn't have.

Gretchen frowned, then squared her shoulders. "Bill died about a year ago. Pneumonia."

"Oh," was all Fargo could think of to say. Her countenance, for a moment, reflected profound emotional pain. He promptly changed the subject. "I take it you're on your way to Oregon, yet I seem to recollect that you once told me you'd never leave St. Louis."

"St. Louis is where Bill died. I couldn't take the bitter memories any longer," Gretchen said, and mustered a wan smile. "I hope to start all over in Oregon. Bill's sister lives out there with her family and she's offered to take me in for a while. We're real close."

"You're traveling all the way to the Oregon Territory by yourself?" Fargo asked in surprise. The journey was a grueling ordeal of stamina and courage, and many settlers succumbed to the varied dangers along the route.

"You kow me," Gretchen said. "When I get it in my head to do something, I do it and hang the consequences."

Fargo recalled she always did have an independent streak a mile wide. He simply nodded.

"How long before you leave?" Gretchen inquired.

"Two hours at the most."

Gretchen looked at his empty coffee cup and the corners of her mouth curled upward slightly. "I heard a shout and came out to investigate. Was that your lathered stallion I saw Davis leading off?"

Fargo nodded.

"Then you've ridden a far piece and must be hungry enough to eat a bear. How would you like some grub?"

The mere mention of food caused Fargo's stomach to rumble. Gretchen heard it and brightened.

"Come to my wagon and I'll fix you a quick meal," she offered.

Skye hesitated for all of two seconds. He *was* famished, and a hot meal would revitalize him for the long return trip. "I'd be obliged," he said.

"And while you're eating," Webber interjected, "I'll see if I can round up some men to go with you."

"Don't bother," Fargo told him.

"But what if you run into hostiles?" Webber protested. "And you'll need help when you catch up with Blue Raven."

"I'll handle it myself," Fargo said. The settler appeared confused so Fargo elaborated. "One man has a better chance of taking Blue Raven by surprise than a small army. The more men I take along, the more likely that crafty renegade will spot us coming and give us the slip. And let's face it. The men here aren't accustomed to Indian-style fighting.

Hell, I bet most of them have never even killed a man."

Webber scratched his chin. "I can't say as I like the idea of letting you ride off alone, but you're right. The only man on this train who has ever killed someone is Calhoun."

"You know that for a fact?" Fargo inquired.

"Sure do," Webber said, and one of the others grunted assent. "We didn't know it at the time, but he'd gunned down two men in Independence a few days before he caught up with us at the Missouri border and asked to tag along." He paused and peered into the darkness to the north. "It turns out he accused a man named Bowdrie of cheating at cards. Bowdrie and a friend went for their guns and Calhoun shot them dead on the spot."

"How did you learn all this?" Fargo wondered.

"Bowdrie's two brothers and another man showed up yesterday," Webber said grimly. "They want to even the score. When they found out Calhoun wasn't here, they were fit to be tied." He sighed. "They're camped a ways north of our wagons. I reckon there will be blood spilled when Calhoun gets back."

Fargo now understood the reason the gambler had joined the wagon train. Calhoun must have figured Bowdrie's kin would want revenge. So, either to avoid further bloodshed or because he was afraid of being killed, the gambler had lit out for the Oregon Territory.

"Say, what about that food?" Gretchen asked.

"Lead the way," Fargo said, and walked beside her as she headed south along the line of wagons. He admired the sheen to her hair and the sway of her shapely legs. Thinking of the amorous interlude they'd shared in St. Louis stoked the fire in his organ and he involuntarily became hard. It had been a while since he went to bed with a woman; his body was raring to go. He chided himself for being a horny bastard. Gretchen was a widow and from all indications had changed her youthful rowdy ways. He should accept her meal in the spirit in which it had been offered and not give in to his lustful urges.

"It's wonderful to see you again, Skye," she commented, smiling at him. "I still think of those times we shared every now and then."

"I figured you'd forgotten all about me," Fargo said.

"A woman never forgets a man who fills her to the brim," Gretchen said bluntly.

The big man chuckled. "And a man never forgets a woman who's fun in bed," he said.

Gretchen locked her deep green eyes on his. "Did you ever miss me? Just a little?"

"A lot, at first," Fargo replied. And he had. Never one to let moss grow under him, though, he'd gone on with his life, crisscrossing the West again and again, always on the move and always receptive to the charms of the many females who found his rugged good looks and powerful build irresistible. Or so they'd claimed.

"There's my wagon," Gretchen said, nodding at a prairie schooner ahead spaced fifteen yards from those on both sides.

Fargo regarded the medium-sized wagon, which was nine feet long, four feet wide, and sported sides two feet high, and glanced at her. "You handle this rig all by yourself?"

"Some of the men help on the tough grades," Gretchen said. She came to the back of the wagon and reached up to grip the top of the tail board. Above her reared the curved canvas top, stretched taut on a frame of hickory bows.

"Allow me," Fargo said, gripping her slim waist and giving her a boost inside. His hands slid down her legs as she climbed into the darkened bed.

"Now where did I put that lantern?" she remarked. "I'll help you find it," Fargo volunteered, and clambered inside. He squinted, waited for his eyes to adjust to the dim confines. Piled to his right and left were boxes and crates; spread out on the floor were blankets and a pillows. Gretcher was standing to his left. She suddenly stepped right in front of him.

"Don't be in such a hurry."

Fargo felt her body press flush with his and her lips swoop hungrily to his mouth. He responded automatically, flicking his tongue out to meet hers and reaching up to cup her huge breasts. She voiced a plaintive groan and strained her hips against his thighs. Their kiss lingered for minutes. At last she pulled back.

"Oh, God," Gretchen breathed. "It's been so long. So damn long." She tossed her shawl to the floor.

"What about that food?" Fargo asked with a mischievous grin.

"Can it wait?"

"I don't mind having dessert first," Fargo said, and nuzzled her neck. She cooed and ran her fingers through his hair, knocking off his hat. He sculpted her body with his palms, generating an inferno of heat wherever he touched. Bringing his hands up over her soft things, he heard her sharp intake of breath. Then he cupped her mound and she arched her back.

"Oh! Don't stop. Please."

Fargo wasn't about to. He tongued her throat, his left hand undoing the top of her dress. It parted, permitting her heaving globes to burst forth, and he planted his mouth on an erect nipple.

"Yes!" she breathed.

He lingered at her gorgeous breasts, his right hand stroking slowly between her legs all the while. She gulped in air and trembled. Her musky scent tingled his nostrils as he began to slide to his knees. He raised her dress, exposing those silky legs he recalled so well, and touched his lips to her warm skin above the knee.

Gretchen uttered a tiny moan.

Fargo looped his arms around her and abruptly lifted her into the air. He took a quick stride, then gently deposited her on top of the blankets. Her legs fell open, the dress sliding up to her waist, revealing her white underwear. He gripped the fabric and pulled the panties off. A fierce passion seized him at the sight of her public hair and the moist slit below.

He lowered his face between her thighs and probed her nether lips. At the first contact she whined and clamped her legs to the sides of his head. He found the seat of her sexual pleasure and caressed it with the tip of his tongue.

"Yes, yes . . . oooooooh, yes!"

A slick furnace enfolded Fargo's face. He sucked and licked greedily, feeling his hard spear trying to bust from his pants. Her hands pressed down on his head, trying to bury him in her crack. Her breaths were like the rasping of a steam engine and she squirmed deliciously.

When Fargo could stand the erotic suspense no longer,

he positioned himself and unfastened his britches. She saw his member leap free and reached out to grip the engorged shaft.

"Oh, God! Put it in. I want you inside me."

He aligned his knees, touched the tip off his organ to her slick inner walls, then shoved in to the hilt and felt her buck under him. A gurgling screech started to issue from her contorted lips and she bit down on her left forearm. She was doing her best not to make noise that could be heard beyond the wagon.

Fargo began a rocking motion, an in-and-out rhythm that sent shivers of sheer delight up his spine. Pacing himself, he kissed her face, her neck, and her tits. His hands gripped her glossy buttocks and lifted her to meet his thrusts.

"My magnificent stallion," Gretchen whispered. "Ahhhhhh, yes!"

He pumped and pumped, feeling sweat cake his body, listening to the slap of their damp bodies. She suddenly bit him hard on the shoulder and he nearly cried out. In return he squeezed her breasts until she whimpered in ecstasy. The wagon creaked crazily but he didn't care if she didn't. All that mattered was their union, the blending of their bodies in primal desire.

"Oh, Skye," Gretchen said, and her body thrashed uncontrollably. "It's coming! It's coming! Just a little more."

An intense sensation of pure sensual delirium built at the base of Fargo's maleness and exploded outward. He grasped her hips and drove himself into the core of her being, supporting himself on his palms for greater leverage.

"Oh! Oh! Oh!" Gretchen gasped. "Yesssss!"

They came together, and Fargo kept pounding for as long as his organ stayed hard. Her fingernails bit into his arms. Finally she went limp and her limbs sagged to the blankets. He collapsed on top of her, his right ear on her chest, and heard the frantic beating of her heart.

For the longest time neither of them spoke. Gretchen played with his hair and rubbed the back of his neck. At last she sighed and said, "How about that food I promised you? I wouldn't want you to think I was inhospitable."

Fargo laughed at the notion.

5

An hour and a half later Fargo walked from the wagon feeling mightily refreshed. He was eager to get back in the saddle, and he noted with satisfaction that the Ovaro and four other horses were in readiness near the fire that Webber and eight settlers sat around, conversing. Apparently word of his arrival had spread. The men looked up as he approached and Webber stood.

"Your pinto is all set to go."

"So I see," Fargo said, walking straight to the stallion. He rubbed its neck, checked the cinch on his saddle, and verified that the Sharps was loaded. Then he untied the old flintlock and extended it toward the temporary wagon-boss. "Here. Maybe someone on the train can use this. I took it off one of Blue Raven's men."

Webber took the rifle. "I sure wish you would change your mind about taking some of us along."

"No," Fargo stated, and gripped the reins. He gazed up at the stars, estimating the time and the distance he had to cover. "Be looking for Purdy and Calhoun to show before nightfall."

A gruff voice abruptly spoke up, causing all of the settlers to freeze in place. "So it's true. You know where the son of a bitch is at."

Shifting, Fargo laid eyes on three men who were walking toward the fire from the north. None were settlers. The man in the lead was big—as big as Skye—and wore a gun on each hip. Black hair hung to the man's shoulders and a drooping mustache adorned his upper lip under a hooked nose. He wore a black hat low over his eyes.

"I'm Dell Bowdrie," the man announced without ceremony. He jabbed a finger at a shorter version of himself on the left. "This is my brother, Tick." His other hand motioned at the third man. "And Pony Banner."

"Skye Fargo."

"So we heard," Bowdrie said. "Somebody told us you can lead us to Wes Calhoun."

Webber blurted out, "Who did?"

"None of your business," Bowdrie replied, his gaze never leaving the Trailsman. His thumbs were hooked in his belt, his posture deceptively relaxed. "We have a score to settle with Calhoun, Fargo. He killed kin of ours. I want you to take us to him."

"I ride alone," Fargo said, taking an immediate dislike to the Bowdrie brothers and their pard. They were hardcases, saloon sorts who probably shunned honest work unless they were dead broke.

"Not this time," Bowdrie insisted.

Ignoring him, Fargo faced the Ovaro. The crunch of boots on the dry ground alerted him to Bowdrie's approach a moment before a heavy hand fell on his left shoulder and started to spin him around. He went with the motion, offering no resistance, balling his right fist as he whirled.

"Don't turn your—" Dell Bowdrie began angrily.

And then Fargo was all the way around and driving his fist into the hardcase's gut, doubling Bowdrie over. He swiftly delivered a left uppercut to Bowdrie's jaw, his knuckles landing with jarring force. The blow rocked Bowdrie on his heels and sent him staggering backward.

Tick Bowdrie and Pony Banner both went for their hog-legs.

Skye was faster. His right arm a blur, the .44 cleared leather, and both men heard the click of the hammer as he extended the barrel. They instantly became statues, each man with his gun partly drawn. They were staring death in the face and knew it. "Touch sky or die," he barked.

The two men let go of their revolvers and elevated their arms with amazing alacrity.

"Don't shoot, mister," Banner said. "We don't want no trouble with you."

Fargo glanced at Dell Bowdrie. The man stood stooped over, his left hand pressed to his mouth, his right to his stomach. Blood ran down Bowdrie's fingers and dripped from the tip of his chin.

"Damn you!" Dell snapped, the words muffled by his

42

fingers, hatred flashing from his eyes. "No one lays a hand on me."

"That works both ways," Fargo said. He held the Colt steady and mounted the pinto. "If I were you gents, I'd ride on out and forget all about Wes Calhoun. He's a better man than all three of you combined."

"He killed our brother," Tick Bowdrie declared. "We can't let it drop."

"Your choice," Fargo said. "And really none of my affair unless you interfere in *my* business." He gazed meaningfully at each of them. "When I said I ride alone, I meant it. If I see any of you on my back trail, I'll give you a firsthand demonstration of why the Sharps rifle is the best buffalo gun sold."

All three looked at the rifle in the Trailsman's case. They all knew the reputation of the large caliber rifle. In the hands of a competent marksman, a Sharps could down a buffalo or a man at a distance of three hundred yards with ease. Even four and five hundred yard shots had been achieved. And there were those who claimed the Sharps was capable of killing at twice that range. "Shoot a Sharps today," the oldtimers would state with a straight face, "and it will kill tomorrow."

"You don't scare us none, Fargo," Dell Bowdrie growled. "This ain't over until we end it."

Fargo didn't like the idea of having the hardcases dog his trail. He would have enough on his hands simply rescuing Susan Chambers. In the hope of provoking Dell Bowdrie into drawing and finishing the matter right there, he commented sarcastically, "Some men don't have the sense God gave a jackass."

Dell flushed with spite but made no move for his gun.

Scowling, Fargo wagged the .44. "Take a hike. And keep those arms where I can see them until you're out of sight."

The trio walked slowly northward, casting steely glances over their shoulders. They prudently held their hands away from their sidearms.

"Those gents will hate you for life," Webber commented when they were out of earshot.

Fargo shrugged. "A man who never makes enemies

doesn't have the backbone to deserve the handle," he said. He waited until the three men were dozens of yards off before sliding the .44 into its holster.

"You'd best skedaddle before they find their gumption," Webber recommended and stepped forward. "Here." He held up the lead to the four saddled mounts.

"Thanks," Fargo said, taking it in his left hand. "I'll be back as soon as I can with the Chambers gal. Figure a week or thereabouts, if nothing goes wrong."

"We'll be here," Webber promised.

With a nod Fargo rode out, heading eastward, the four horses obediently following several yards to his rear. He could tell by the Ovaro's steady gait that the stallion had benefited from the brief rest. Which was good, because considering what lay in store for them, they would be getting little rest for the next few days.

He rode half a mile before cutting northward. Stars still dominated the firmament and he calculated it would be another hour before daylight. A brisk, invigorating breeze cooled his face and neck. The picturesque, tranquil setting, with a sea of waving grassland stretching before him and majestic mountains in the distance, stirred his soul, reminding him of yet another reason he preferred the outdoors to the dubious charms of so-called civilization. He felt at home in the unfettered wild, whereas cites, where people were kept in line by countless laws and rules, where bricks and stones replaced trees and the nurturing earth, were like cages without bars.

After another thirty minutes of riding, Fargo slanted to the northeast. He knew that sooner or later he would find the Green River. Once he did, he would follow it until he rejoined Calhoun and the others. Typical night sounds assailed his ears. Once, far to the northwest, a wolf howled plaintively. Later, much closer a bobcat screeched. And just as the dank scent of water reached his nostrils, he heard the throaty snarl of a mountain lion to his south.

Shortly thereafter Fargo found the river. In the moonlight locating an especially shallow point at which to cross was easy, and he was soon riding northward along the east bank. Not withstanding the dense brush, he made excellent time.

Dawn's rosy fingers gradually speared above the horizon, well in advance of the fiery orb that eventually peeked down to greet the wildlife stirring from sleep.

Many animals came to the river to satisfy their thirst. Fargo saw deer, buffalo, elk, and antelope. He spied rabbits, raccoons, and a fox. The land teemed with game, a hunter's paradise. He could have shot whatever creature he desired for his breakfast, but he pressed onward in his eagerness to deliver the mounts and head out after the Chambers woman.

Fargo idly noted the passage of the hours. The sun rose higher. He pushed the stallion harder since he could see the ground and avoid potential obstacles. Twice he stopped to water the animals sparingly, knowing full well they would drink until they became loggy if he didn't.

He was several miles from the point where he expected to rejoin the others when he heard the gunfire. His head snapped up at the sound of the faint retort of rifles and the fainter crack of pistols. Fierce whoops attended the shooting. Spuring the pinto into a gallop, he tugged on the lead to get the four mounts to keep pace.

The whoops told him that his worst fears had been realized. He'd known all along that he should assist the four men before going after Susan Chambers because the odds were high that they would be discovered by a passing war party. And since men on foot could never hope to flee from Indians possessed of fleet horses, Calhoun and the others were as good as dead unless he helped them.

The battle continued, the noise growing louder by the second. Fargo took that as a good sign. Once the shooting ceased, it meant the Indians had prevailed. He threaded among stands of trees bordering the water's edge until he spotted men on horseback ahead. Then he took the four mounts into a thicket and tied the lead securely before venturing closer to the fight.

A single glance identified the warriors as Utes, a tribe that inhabited a section of the Rockies much farther south but who were known to frequently send raiding parties into the Wind River region. He counted nine, three of whom were dead on the ground near a thin copse where the defenders had made their stand.

Fargo frowned in disapproval of the site where Purdy and company were concealed. Except for a few trees, there was inadequate cover to protect the settlers and the gambler from the arrows and bullets the Indians were pouring into the brush. He saw a body sprawled at the base of the bush and believed it to be Flanders.

Then a disturbing fact became apparent. He realized that only one gun was holding the Indians at bay, a single pistol being fired from behind a tree. A black hat popped into view as the man sent a shot into an Ute and toppled the warrior to the ground.

Calhoun!

Fargo yanked out the Sharps and moved into the open. The copse lay thirty yards away. None of the Utes had yet noticed his arrival. Using his thumb, he cocked the hammer and tucked the heavy stock to his right shoulder. One of the Indians held a rifle, which qualified him as the most dangerous. Fargo took a bead on the Ute's torso, touched his finger to the trigger and fired.

At the boom of the Sharps the Ute threw his arms into the air and fell.

Working swiftly, Fargo fed in another cartridge, pulled back the hammer, and aimed at a burly warrior wielding a bow. The Ute turned to look at him and he sent a slug into the center of the man's face. Two down, four to go, he reflected, inserting yet a third round into the chamber.

Now the remaining members of the war party were aware of the firing from their flank. They stopped or wheeled their horses, and as they did, Wes Calhoun glided from behind the trees and squeezed off three shots in rapid succession. Two of the Utes dropped even as the last pair yipped and charged the Trailsman.

Fargo had to force himself not to hurry. He raised the rifle and sighted on a brave with an arrow nocked to a bow string. Well aware that Indian archers were adept at hitting a target dead center at one hundred yards, he sighted on the man's chest at the selfsame instant the Ute sighted on him. He fired a hair before the warrior did.

The Ute catapulted off the rear of his steed, the bow falling from his limp fingers.

As if in slow motion Fargo watched the spinning shaft fly toward him. He glimpsed the glittering tip and the revolving feathers. Instinctively, he hunched low in the saddle and listened to the buzzing of the arrow as it passed within inches of the crown of his hat.

Straightening, Skye clasped the Sharps in his left hand, released the reins, and whipped the Colt clear. The final brave swung a war club high overhead and vented a savage yell. Undaunted, Skye shot twice, hit twice, and felt grim satisfaction when the Ute fell.

He headed for the copse. None of the Utes were moving. Most had puddles of blood under them. He replaced the rifle in the case but held on to the Colt, unwilling to take any chances. Near the river on the west side of the copse was another corpse he recognized; Seth Purdy, face down in the dirt, three arrows in his back.

Calhoun was standing with his back to the tree, reloading. His fingers were giving him problems, however, and he fumbled with the cartridges. The arm holding the revolver kept drooping.

"Where's the boy?" Fargo called out when still fifteen yards off.

The gambler twisted and pointed to his left.

Dismay washed over Fargo as he laid eyes on Adam Purdy. The youth lay on his back near a small boulder, a crimson trickle flowing from a gaping hole in the side of his neck. "Damn," Fargo muttered, and glanced at Calhoun. "What about you? Are you all right?"

"I reckon not," Calhoun said, mustering a wan smile. Then he stiffened and pitched onto his face.

6

Fargo had just finished burying the Purdys and Ed Flanders and was walking toward the small fire he'd started on the east side of the copse when Wes Calhoun revived. He saw the gambler stir, then blink and try to sit up. "You should take it easy for a spell," he advised.

Calhoun grunted and lay back down. He inspected the crude white bandage on his left side below the shoulder, then looked at his shirt, coat, and hat lying in a bundle near the fire only a yard from his side. "Thanks for patching me up," he said.

"You bled a lot, but the bullet didn't come close to the heart or the lungs," Fargo disclosed, halting and kneeling so he could feed another branch into the flames. It had taken him the better part of an hour to gingerly probe the bullet hole with his fingers and remove the slug, then to cauterize the hole with a red-hot brand.

"I owe you," Calhoun said gratefully. "If you hadn't come along when you did, I'd be raven bait about now and some Ute would be showing my hair to his wife and boasting of the kill."

"Are you up to telling me what happened?"

Calhoun nodded and licked his lips. "We stayed with the buffalo all last night. Purdy insisted on eating steaks for breakfast. He even made a fire where we were, out in the open." He sighed and gazed at the sky. "I tried to talk him out of it, but he was as hardheaded as a mule."

Bowing his head, Fargo imagined the result. The band of Utes had seen the smoke from afar and ridden to investigate. They would have bided their time until the right moment, then attacked.

"We ate and headed west, as you'd told us to do," Calhoun went on sadly. "When we came to the river, Purdy wanted to build another fire and try to catch fish for our midday meal.

I told him if he set so much as one blade of grass alight, I'd shoot him."

Fargo looked up in surprise. "Did you know there were Indians about?"

"No. But I'd had this nagging feeling all morning," Calhoun said. "Like I do when I'm holding a full house and the guy across the table is trying not to show it but it's plain he's holding four of a kind. I knew something was wrong."

"What then?"

"I wanted to get under cover in the trees," Calhoun related. "But Purdy wouldn't listen. He headed for the water to try his hand at fishing. That's when the sons of bitches hit us. Purdy went down without firing a shot. Flanders was killed a minute later."

Fargo saw the gambler's features darken.

"Adam and me held our own for a while, then Adam took a bullet," Calhoun said quietly. "I tried to go to him and got shot myself. Started bleeding like a stuck pig. But I wasn't about to let those painted devils get me without a fight." He grinned wryly. "I was on my last legs when you showed up."

"Just luck," Fargo stated honestly and glanced to his left where the Ovaro and the four new mounts were ground-hitched. Now there were three horses too many, and the extra animals gave him the germ of an idea.

"I've learned a valuable lesson out of all this," Calhoun said. "Never, ever, get stranded in Indian country with a greenhorn from the East."

Fargo nodded. "Farmers may know crops, but they don't know beans about fighting hostiles."

Putting his right hand on the ground, Calhoun grit his teeth and succeeded in sitting up. "So what will you do now? Go after the woman?"

"I'd like to," Fargo admitted, "but I have a bit of a problem."

"Me?" Calhoun said. "Don't fret yourself. I'll take one of those horses and head for the wagon train as soon as I'm able."

"There are two problems with that," Fargo noted. "First, there might be more Utes in the area, or maybe a band of

49

Sioux or Cheyenne. If they heard the shots, they'll show up sooner or later. It wouldn't be too smart for you to stay here any length of time in the shape you're in."

"What's the second problem?"

"Three hardcases who go by the names of Dell and Tick Bowdrie, and Pony Banner. They're waiting for you at the wagon train."

Calhoun went rigid, then swallowed hard. He looked down at his revolver, his forehead creasing in deep thought. "I reckon I should have expected it."

"They tried to make me bring them here," Fargo mentioned.

The gambler glanced at the big man. "And you turned them down? I bet they didn't like that."

"Let's just say I'll have to watch my back for a while," Fargo said.

"You've read them right," Calhoun confirmed. "The Bowdries are notorious back shooters. Anyone who tangles with them winds up with a bullet between the shoulder blades. The law would have hung them long ago if there had been any evidence that could be used in court." He paused. "I should have known better than to call Frank Bowdrie a cheat."

"Was he?"

"The biggest damn cheat in Missouri. I caught him dealing from the bottom of the deck and accused him in front of an entire saloon. Naturally he went for his gun. So did a partner of his," Calhoun said.

"I heard you killed them both," Fargo commented.

Calhoun nodded. "Then I got to thinking. I knew Dell and Tick would be after me as soon as they found out. Since I didn't much like the notion of being bushwhacked, I figured I'd make tracks for the Oregon Territory."

"Sometimes it's a lot wiser to pull freight than your gun," Fargo said politely and received a sharp look in rebuke.

"Wiser, hell!" Calhoun snapped. "The plain truth is that I lost my nerve, and you know it. A yellow streak sprouted down my spine. I couldn't stand the idea of always having to keep my back to the wall, of never knowing when Dell

Bowdrie would make his play. So I ran," he concluded in disgust.

Fargo made no comment. He knew that courage and cowardice were two sides of the same coin. A man could be courageous all his life and then one day a set of circumstances might develop that would cause the same man to turn tail. It didn't necessarily brand the man as a chronic coward. He'd known soldiers, mountain men, and Indians it had happened to, and most of them regained their self-respect by confronting the next danger head-on.

"It's been eating at me ever since," Calhoun continued. "The farther the wagon train went, the worse I felt. When Susan Chambers was taken and Purdy wanted to go after her, I figured I could prove something to myself by going along. I wanted to show that I have true grit."

Skye nodded toward the dead Utes. "I'd say you've proven your point."

"Have I?" Calhoun said doubtfully.

"No man is cast in iron," Fargo noted. "If twenty or thirty more Utes were to come riding toward us right this minute, I'd have us both in the saddle and on our way south before they so much as blinked."

"That's different," Calhoun said. "That's just common sense."

Fargo realized there was nothing he could say that would make the gambler feel any better. Calhoun's problem was too personal, a crisis of the soul; he had to come to terms with his own conscience.

"Well," Calhoun said, "it's a cinch I can't go back to the wagon train in this condition. I reckon you should just leave me here. I'll get by."

"No," Fargo said. "It's too risky. I'm taking you with me."

"I'd only slow you down."

"Not that much," Fargo disagreed, rising. "And if you want a chance to prove yourself, here it is. Rescuing the Chambers woman won't be easy. Blue Raven might wind up taking both our scalps. But we've got to head out. I can't put off going after her any longer."

Calhoun stared at the horses, then at his chest. He reached up and touched the bandage. "I'm sore as hell, but I suppose I can hold up."

Fargo grinned. "I'll tie you in the saddle if you fall off too many times."

"That's nice to know," Calhoun said, smiling. He ran his fingers over the bandage and his forehead became furrowed. "This fabric feels like silk, What did you use, anyway?"

"Your shirt sleeves."

"What?" Calhoun said, and grabbed his shirt from the bundle. His mouth dropped at seeing that both sleeves had been cut off. "You lunkhead. Do you have any idea how much shirts like this cost?"

Laughing, Fargo walked to the horses. "Would you rather have bled to death?" he responded.

"Of course not," Calhoun muttered, and sighed. "I just hope the next time I'm shot, there's a sawbones around."

Fargo brought the animals over. "Get dressed. We'll stick to the river as far as we can so you'll be able to wash that wound every few hours or so." He removed the first horse from the string, then wrapped the weapons he'd collected from the Purdys and Flanders in a blanket and secured the bundle to the last mount in the line. By the time he finished, the gambler had donned the clothes. With the frock coat on, no one could tell the shirt sleeves were missing. "All set?"

Calhoun nodded, patted his revolver, and stepped to the horse Fargo had removed. He held his left arm close to his chest, gripped the saddle horn with his right hand, stuck a foot in the stirrup and pulled himself up. His face flushed with the effort and he swayed as he straightened. Then he steadied himself, inhaling deeply.

After kicking dirt onto the fire, Fargo swung onto the Ovaro and turned northward. He saw several of the Indian mounts grazing off to the east but didn't bother trying to catch them. Not only would it waste more precious time, but he had enough spare horses for his purpose. With the gurgling river at his left, he spurred the stallion forward.

The gambler fell in beside Fargo on the right. "I'll hold you to your promise to tie me to the saddle if I fall down," he said.

"Feeling weak?"

"Feeling sick," Calhoun said.

Fargo was ready to lend a hand if necessary, but Calhoun resolutely forged onward. He admired the gambler's gumption in holding up so well. Approximately ten miles from the copse he halted to give Calhoun a short breather and let the horses drink a little. Then they resumed their journey, sticking to the open land that bordered the trees and brush where they could make better time.

The sun hung an hour or so above the western horizon when Fargo spotted buzzards circling the east bank a mile ahead. He guessed the carrion eaters had found the Sioux he'd slain the day before, although it was unusual for the big, ugly birds to land amidst trees. Vultures preferred open land where they could see predators coming and take wing immediately.

As Fargo drew closer he saw five or six of the buzzards clustered around something near the water's edge, not in the stand of trees where the brave's body lay. What had they found? he wondered, his blue eyes narrowing.

"Any idea what those birds have found?" Calhoun asked.

Skye related his fight with the wounded Sioux and ended with, "But it can't be him. The body was in the trees and there's no way buzzards can haul a full-grown man anywhere."

"Maybe it's an animal," Calhoun guessed.

The large brownish-black birds became aware of the approaching horses and raised their bald, wrinkled red heads from their feeding, several with grisly strips of flesh dangling from their powerful beaks. They stubbornly held their ground until the horses were a dozen yards away, then rose into the air with much ponderous flapping of their long wings. One hissed angrily at the intrusion on their feast.

"Never did like those critters," Calhoun commented distastefully.

Fargo had once shared the gambler's revulsion until an old Shoshoni, a wise warrior who had counted more coup as a young man than any other member of the tribe and later went on to become a revered chief, impressed on him the idea that all animals had a reason for living. The buffalo were put on earth so the Indians would have food to eat and lodges in which to live. Deer, antelope, and other game were equally important. Even critters few liked filled a need. Skunks, the old Shoshoni had claimed with a twinkle in his eyes, made humans better appreciate flowers. Rattlesnakes taught humans to tread carefully. And buzzards make people grateful that they weren't born birds. The memory sparked a grin.

As the last of the buzzards took wing, Fargo saw the remains on which they had been feeding. He was surprised to discover an Indian lying there. The man's face, neck, and stomach had been partially consumed. He reined up a few feet off and dismounted.

"Now I feel even sicker," Calhoun remarked.

Scarcely breathing because of the stench, Fargo stepped up to the corpse. It was impossible to determine if the warrior was the same brave he'd slain, although the size and general build were similar. Suddenly he realized that the buzzards had not been the only creatures eating the body. Great bites had been taken out of the abdomen and the neck bore tooth marks in addition to the gashes caused by pecking beaks. Then he glanced at the soil beyond the corpse and felt goose bumps break out on his skin.

Clearly imprinted in the earth were enormous paw prints, the claws and pads remarkably distinct. The tracks were so large that only one type of animal could have made them.

"Grizzly," Fargo said softly, and spied drag marks leading from the trees to the brave. He concluded that one of the great bears had found the corpse and dragged it to the bank where the buzzards spotted it. But why hadn't the bear consumed the entire body? Had it fed recently and not been hungry? He knew that grizzlies seldom strayed far from kills and glanced at the woods in consternation.

"Did you say grizzly?" Calhoun asked anxiously.

Before Skye could answer, a terrible roar rent the air and a huge brown shape appeared in the woods, crashing through the trees toward them.

7

Fargo glimpsed the twelve-hundred pound brute's massive head, slavering jaws, and prominent hump above its rippling shoulders, and then he whirled and dashed toward the Ovaro, intending to grab the Sharps. But the stallion and the rest of the horses panicked, shying away from the onrushing beast. Fargo seized the Ovaro's reins before it could bolt and dug in his heels. One look over his shoulder told him that he'd never reach the rifle in time.

The ponderous monster burst from cover and paused, glancing at the rearing, neighing horses.

Calhoun was trying to bring his mount under control. In his weakened condition he could barely hold on and the horse headed toward the stand.

Unexpectedly the grizzly lunged, closing on the gambler's horse and swinging a huge paw that caught the mount full on the side of the head. The horse went down in midstride, blood spraying in all directions, falling forward onto its head and neck and rolling.

Fargo saw Calhoun throw himself from the saddle just in time and land on the side, away from the bear. In desperation he lunged and grasped the Ovaro's bridle. The pinto dragged him backward, its eyes wide, its instinctive fear supplanting its loyalty. He managed to get a hold on the saddle and snatched at the Sharps, his fingers closing on the stock.

A shot blasted.

Twisting, Fargo discovered the grizzly had its front paws on the gambler's now motionless horse and was glaring at Calhoun, who had pulled his revolver and fired while flat on his back. The pearl-handled Colt spoke twice more, smoke blossoming from the barrel, and the grizzly's head snapped up. The brute focused on Calhoun and moved toward him.

Inflamed with concern for the gambler, Fargo frantically tugged on the rifle and pulled it free. He swung around, inserting a cartridge as rapidly as his fingers could move, hearing Calhoun fire two more times. The grizzly seemed unfazed, its thick skull impervious to the .44.

Justifiably, grizzly bears were rated the most temperamental, fierce, and tenacious animals in all the West. As Lewis and Clark had noted decades ago, grizzlies were notoriously hard to kill. Even flintlocks at close range had often been unable to down the monsters. And using a revolver on a grizzly was the same as using a slingshot on a buffalo; neither did a damn bit of good.

A Sharps, however, could slay either with one shot provided that shot was well placed. No one knew better than Fargo. With the grizzly almost on top of Calhoun, he threw caution to the winds and ran up to the bear, extending the rifle as he did. The grizzly detected him and began to turn its head. In a final leap, Fargo jammed the Sharps into the bear's right ear and fired. He expected the grizzly would drop on the spot. Instead, it staggered sideways, then reared onto its hind legs.

Suddenly fargo found himself staring up at an enraged bestial colossus, an empty rifle in his hands. Calhoun fired one last shot. The grizzly opened its horrible maw, exposing tapered teeth that could crush bone with a single bite. Fargo swooped his right hand to his Colt, but the barrel was just flashing from the holster when the bear shuffled rearward, then crashed to the ground on its back.

Fearing that the brute might have some life left, Fargo snapped off two shots, aiming at its right eye. The bear lay still, its mouth still open, its great limbs limp. He cautiously moved nearer, watching the bear's sides to see if it was breathing. Up close the formidable beast seemed almost indestructible. He studied its bleeding face and neck, satisfied the Sharps had done the job.

"Thanks," Calhoun said, pushing to his feet. His face was pale and he winced as he stood. "That's twice you've saved my hide."

"Maybe one day you can do the same for me," Fargo said absently, holstering the .44. He turned to the stricken horse. The grizzly's paw had split its head as a hammer would an overripe melon. Brains and blood oozed from an inch-wide crack in the mount's skull.

"Thank God that wasn't me," Calhoun said.

Fargo looked at him. A red stain had developed on Calhoun's shirt front above the bandage. "Are you all right?" he asked.

The gambler looked down at himself and scowled. "I'm bleeding again but no bones are broken."

Swiveling, Fargo saw the Ovaro fifteen yards away. The stallion had mastered its fear after fleeing a short distance. But the three other horses were forty yards off at the edge of dense woods. The lead had become entangled in heavy brush, halting their flight. He went to the pinto, replaced the rifle, and forked leather. "Be back in a minute," he said.

The three mounts behaved skittishly as Fargo rode toward them. If not for the tangled lead, he reflected, they would be on their way to Mexico. He spoke soothingly to them as he neared the woods, then slid down and freed the lead. Reassured by his presence and his tone, the horses quickly calmed down. He climbed on the Ovaro and returned to Calhoun.

The gambler had removed his frock coat and shirt and was washing the bandage in the Green River. He breathed heavily, blood seeping from the charred hole high on his chest. "After I settle affairs with the Bowdries, I may head for Denver and live there the rest of my days," he commented. "I don't know how you do it."

"Do what?" Fargo replied.

"Live out here," Calhoun said, nodding at the tract of prairie and mountains to the west. "It's too wild for my taste, what with the Indians and the critters out to kill you every chance they get. Give me a saloon any day. A stiff whiskey, a willing filly, and a royal flush are my kind of excitement."

"I like to drink as much as the next man," Fargo said. "And I've never said no to a woman yet." He gazed out over the scenic countryside. "But this is what I like the best. Living off the land and being obligated to no one. The wide open spaces get in a man's blood, Wes."

"I suppose," Calhoun said. "But give me soft sheets and a pillow any day to sleeping on the hard ground. I wasn't cut out to be a scout or an Indian fighter."

"Then we'd better be heading out. Indians might have heard our gunshots and come to investigate."

The reminder goaded the gambler to move faster. He finished washing the bandage, let Fargo tie it, and put on the rest of his clothes. A second horse was removed from the string and he climbed into the saddle. "Lead the way, pard."

Fargo continued northward along the river. He figured that the renegades had stuck close to the water so their mounts and the horses they'd stolen could drink frequently. His deduction proved accurate. He found their tracks paralleling the river, the same trail of shod and unshod animals he'd pursued the day before. The prints weren't as distinct but they were still clear enough to easily follow.

The hours passed agreeably. Calhoun became talkative, and Fargo listened to the gambler tell of his childhood on a farm in Pennsylvania, his running off at the age of seventeen after he killed a rival for a woman's affection in a fist fight, and how Calhoun was later introduced to the gambling trade in New Orleans by a professional cardsharp.

"Talk about getting in a man's blood," Calhoun concluded. "I was fresh off the farm, and there I was up to my eyebrows in perfumed ladies, wearing the finest clothes, and drinking the best liquor money could buy. It had never occurred to me that a man could make a living that way."

"Ever go back to Pennsylvania?" Fargo idly inquired while alertly scanning the area ahead.

"No," Calhoun said rather sadly. "I reckon my folks and my sister figure I'm dead by now, and I see no cause to disillusion them." He paused. "If they knew what I do for a living, they'd be heartbroken. To them, I'd be an outright sinner."

Fargo said nothing. He'd known his share of God-fearing folk in his time and knew how strait-laced they could be. In a way he felt sorry for Calhoun.

The sun dipped steadily lower in the blue vault of the sky, and when it was just above the western horizon Fargo decided to halt for the night. Had he been by himself, he would have kept going. But Calhoun needed the rest, and he'd grown to like the easygoing gambler. They made their camp in a ravine where their fire would be shielded from view, and Fargo used his throwing knife to bag a rabbit for their supper.

"You're right handy with that toothpick," Calhoun commented after witnessing the twenty-foot throw.

"Lots of practice," Fargo said. He proceeded to skin the animal and prepared a crude spit to roast it on. The delicious aroma of the succulent meat made his mouth water. He hadn't realized how hungry he was, and he wasn't alone.

"Too bad you didn't kill a bull elk," Calhoun said. "I could eat one, bones and all."

"I'll be sure and hunt for one tomorrow," Fargo said dryly. "Unless you'd rather do the honors."

"Me?" Calhoun said, and snorted. "Brother, if you leave the hunting up to me, we'll both starve."

Fargo chuckled. "Then I'll do the hunting. But we won't be eating elk or deer or buffalo or anything big."

"Why not?"

"Because from here on out all killing must be done quietly," Fargo said. "A shot can carry for a mile or so, and we don't want anyone to know we're in this neck of the woods. Indians or renegades."

The gambler pondered for a bit. "How much of a lead do you reckon Blue Raven has on us?"

"It depends on how hard he's been traveling," Fargo answered. "It's been three days since the attack on the wagons. I figure he pushed it the first day or so, then slowed up."

"Why?"

"He sent half of his men to check his backtrail, remember?" Fargo reminded him. "He wouldn't want to get too far ahead of them so they could catch up easily."

"Even so, it'll take us four days, probably more, to overtake the band," Calhoun deduced.

"That's about right," Fargo said.

Calhoun placed his right palm on his chest. "Figures," he muttered, and squared his shoulders. "Don't worry about me. I'll keep up."

"I'm more concerned about the horses," Fargo said. "This kind of country is rough on a horse and we've got

59

a long ways to go. That's the reason I brought the extra mounts along. We'll take turns riding them so they don't become too tuckered out. Two hours an animal should be about right.''

"Relays, huh?'' Calhoun said, nodding. "It's a smart plan. Should help us catch those murdering vermin that much sooner.''

"I just hope Susan Chambers is still alive when we do,'' Fargo mentioned, and concentrated on cooking the rabbit.

"You're not the only one.''

Almost every waking hour of the next two days was spent in the saddle. The relay idea enabled the horses to travel farther and at a faster pace than they would have otherwise. Blue Raven's men had stayed near the Green River as it wound into the foothills bordering the Wind River range to the east and the Gros Ventre Mountains on the west.

Fargo was pleased with their progress and impressed by Calhoun's endurance. He knew the gambler was in great pain, yet Calhoun never once complained or asked to go slower.

The morning of the third day found them deep in the mountains. On both sides reared stark peaks crowned with snow. Forests of evergreens teeming with abundant wildlife flanked the river. Fargo was in the lead, keeping one eye on the terrain and another on the tracks, when he suddenly noticed the band had changed direction, slanting to the northeast. He reined up and leaned down to inspect the prints.

"What is it?'' Calhoun inquired.

Fargo straightened and pointed. "They're heading into the Wind River range.''

"Prime Indian country, I hear.''

"Indians. Grizzlies. You name it.''

"I think I'd rather face the Bowdrie brothers.''

The trail wound along a series of verdant valleys, going ever deeper into pristine wilderness. Several hours later, Fargo spied a large clearing ahead and halted. At the center was the blackened remains of a campfire. "Stay here,'' he said, drawing the Colt. He rode slowly forward. Tracks were everywhere, and from the number of footprints, he calculated that this was the spot where Blue Raven had waited for the rest of his men to rejoin the band. But they were clearly long gone. He went to the burnt remnants of the fire and slid down. From the depth of the burnt cinders, he figured that Blue Raven had camped there for at least two days awaiting his men.

Fargo stood and slid the .44 into his holster. How far ahead were they now? he wondered. Certainly a day, perhaps two. He frowned and mounted, then motioned for Calhoun to come on. From here on out, he reflected, he would push the horses to their limits.

From the camp the trail led ever deeper into the mountains. For a while it bordered a narrow stream, then crossed a ridge to a lake. Fargo became convinced that Blue Raven or one of the other killers knew the land well.

Leaving the lake, Skye followed a straight course to the base of the bald mountains, swung to the east around its base, and came to a spacious plain ringed by high peaks. As he halted to arch his spine and stretch, he spotted tendrils of black and gray smoke spiraling upward a half-mile distant.

Calhoun saw it also. "Do you think it's them?"

"Let's find out," Fargo said, spurring the Ovaro into a gallop. They had been taking turns leading the spare animals and Calhoun was currently handling the chore. Consequently, Fargo pulled out in front and was the first to see the smoldering skeletal ruins of five tepees situated close to a spring. He also saw the bodies.

Slowing, Fargo pulled the Colt, his eyes flicking right and left. The renegades were gone, but not by more than an hour or so if the fresh tracks were any indication. He counted sixteen bodies; warriors, women, and children who had been shot, stabbed, or trampled to death. Most had also been mutilated. The men were missing their hair, their exposed pink flesh shriveling in the sunlight. Many of both sexes had an ear, a nose, or fingers missing. One woman's buckskin dress had been slit from top to bottom and her breasts sliced off. The gory scene made him feel queasy.

He pieced together the sequence of events. From the style of dress of the women, and the symbols painted on a broken hide-shield lying in the dirt at the outskirts of the village, he concluded the victims had been a group of Shoshonis. Since a third of the dead were warriors who would ordinarily be off hunting or on raids, it was obvious Blue Raven had hit the village at first light when the men were likely to be present and just rousing themselves from sleep.

Fargo wasn't the least bit surprised that Blue Raven had slaughtered the Shoshonis. While the half-breed hated whites, he wasn't all that fond of Indians, either. Maybe Blue Raven blamed both for the accident of birth that made him an outcast from each society. A small band of Shoshoni would have been ripe for the slaughter. And with everyone in the village slain, who would know?

He stopped and dismounted, the Colt cocked and held level at his waist. Stepping over body after body, he avoided puddles of blood and patches of gore. Nearby lay a camp dog, its brains blown out. He heard Calhoun approaching and paused to look over his shoulder. The gambler looked at him, then *past* him at something and started to shout a warning. At the same moment Fargo heard the patter of rushing feet and a bloodcurdling screech.

8

Fargo whirled, his trigger finger tensed to tighten, and saw a Shoshoni woman running toward him with an upraised knife. She was ten feet off, her face distorted by hatred, dried blood caking her right cheek. Heedless of the gun, she was intent on sinking the knife into him. He fired, but not at her. At the last instant he angled the barrel down and blasted lead into the earth at her feet.

The loud shot startled her, drew her up short. She hesitated, watching the revolver rise and point at her chest.

"I don't want to hurt you but I will if you take another step," Fargo warned.

Recoiling, the woman moved her gaze from his hat to his boots. She said something in Shoshoni.

"I don't speak your tongue," Fargo said. "Do you speak any English?"

She cocked her head, then glanced at Calhoun who had ridden up and swung down. "I speak little English," she said softly.

Fargo pointed at the knife. "Drop it," he directed, and gestured with his free hand to demonstrate his meaning.

The woman regarded him uncertainly. She slowly lowered the weapon, her anxious eyes locked on the Colt.

Taking his cue from her fear, Fargo lowered the revolver at the same time. He guessed she was in her late twenties. She had dark hair down to the small of her back, an oval face, and deep, dark eyes. Her lips were full, her figure the same. When she released the knife, he eased the .44 into its holster. "I will not harm you. Do you understand?"

She quickly replied. "Yes. I am much sorry I tried to kill you. I thought you are one of those who did this," she said and motioned to the carnage.

"What's your name?"

"Badger Woman."

Fargo tapped his chest and stated his name. He turned to Calhoun, who had his hand resting on his revolver, and introduced the gambler. "We're after the renegades who killed your people," he informed her.

Her features clouded. "I hope you kill them all. They are worse than Blackfeet."

The Trailsman knew she had voiced the ultimate insult. The Shoshonis and the Blackfeet hated one another. He saw a thin red line on her right temple and said, "You've been wounded. Let us tend it."

"I am fine," Badger Woman declared. She touched the line, then gazed around her as if in an abrupt daze. Suddenly her eyes fluttered and her knees began to sag.

Fargo reached her in two strides and swept her into his arms. She was a feather, her skin warm to his touch. Her eyes closed and she expelled a breath that caressed his face.

"Is she all right?" Calhoun asked.

"I think she just fainted," Fargo responded. "But we'll play it safe and tend her wound right away."

"What do you want me to do?"

"Tether the horses and start a fire," Fargo instructed him. "Then check the bodies to see if anyone else is alive." He carried the woman a dozen yards to a clear space between two burned tepees and gently deposited her on the ground. Hurrying to the spring, he filled his hat with water and returned. Then he took off his red bandanna, dipped it in the hat, and dabbed at the blood encrusted line—actually a thin crease caused by a bullet.

He glanced up as Calhoun walked over. The gambler carried a load of broken lodge poles, several bearing scorch marks. "I figure Blue Raven spent most of the day here, having his fun with the women and looting anything of value. He can't be more than two hours ahead of us."

Calhoun placed the wood down and frowned as he scanned the village. "We can't let the son of a bitch get away with this. Even if the Chambers woman is dead, we can't simply turn around and ride off. We've got to put an end to his raids. You know that, don't you?"

Fargo nodded grimly. His own sentiments, exactly. The bastard deserved to die. And since no one else had ever gotten this close to Blue Raven's bunch before, it was up to the gambler and him to see that the renegade's days of slaughtering innocents came to a permanent end. He gazed at the woman's smooth, lovely face, pleased they had found her. She would give him the excuse he needed to trick the gambler into letting him take the next step alone.

"I'll get more wood," Calhoun said, walking off.

Cradling the Shoshoni's head in his lap, Fargo felt her forehead with his palm. She didn't appear to have a fever. And since the wound wasn't inflamed, she didn't have an infection. He felt satisfied she would revive soon. Folding the bandanna, he dampened her forehead and temples. She was breathing deeply, her bosom rising and falling. Even as he watched, the rhythm changed and he heard an intake of breath. He looked at her face again and found her eyes open, studying him intently. "Howdy," he said pleasantly to reassure her that he was friendly. "Remember me?"

"The handsome white man," Badger Woman said softly. "Yes."

"You fainted."

"I am very sorry," she responded.

"How are you feeling?" Fargo inquired.

"Better, thank you," Badger Woman said. "The ground was moving fast around and I could not stand."

"That's called being dizzy," Fargo said. "Everything probably caught up with you at once." He noticed that she made no effort to sit up so he continued to stroke her brow with the damp bandanna.

"Feels good," Badger Woman commented. She twisted her head to regard the littered corpses and her eyes promptly moistened. "My mother, my father, my sisters are all dead."

"You are lucky Blue Raven didn't kill you, too," Fargo said.

Hatred twisted Badger Woman's lips downward. "Blue Raven!" she spat. "I saw him laugh as his men killed my people. I saw him ride his horse over a child."

"You recognized him?"

Badger Woman nodded. "I saw him many moons ago at a big gathering of Shoshonis. He came to trade guns and horses." A tear trickled from the corner of her right eye. "He acted like he was our friend."

"How many men were with him?" Fargo asked.

"Eleven. They attacked as the sun was rising," Badger Woman related. "They rode in shooting, killing our warriors and the children. A few of the women were shot, but most were being captured when I ran to the west." She paused. "I looked back and something hit me in the head. I fell in the high grass, then I knew nothing until a while ago."

Fargo listened attentively. She had been extremely lucky. In all the confusion the renegades had overlooked her which was the only reason she was still alive.

"I woke up," Badger Woman went on, "and tried to find someone alive." More tears flowed. "Then I heard horses. I thought Blue Raven was coming back so I lay down with the dead."

"And attacked me when I rode in," Fargo concluded, and leaned down. "There's something important I must know. Did you see a white woman with the renegades?"

Badger Woman answered without hesitation. "Yes. A woman with hair the color of the sun. She was much sad."

A tingle of excitement coursed through Fargo. So Susan Chambers was definitely still alive. "Tell me what you saw," he urged.

"She was there," Badger Woman said, pointing southward. "I saw her as I was running. She was on a mare and had a rope around her neck."

"A rope?"

"Yes. One of Blue Raven's men held the other end."

Fargo's blood boiled. The sons of bitches were leading Chamber around like a dog on a leash. They must be afraid she would try to escape, or possibly she already had. "Were her clothes ripped? Was her top torn in any way?"

Badger Woman had to think for a moment. "No. She wore a brown dress. It was dirty, but not ripped."

Good, Fargo reflected. Maybe, just maybe, they hadn't abused her yet. Suddenly fingers lightly touched his cheek and he glanced down at the Shoshoni.

"You have kind eyes," she said.

"No one ever told me that before," Skye said self-consciously. He saw the gambler returning with wood and put his hands under her shoulders. "Here. Try to sit up."

Rising and smiling enigmatically, Badger Woman let her

fingers linger on his neck before placing both hands in her lap. "You have been kind to me. I will be kind to you."

Wondering if that meant what he thought it meant, Fargo stood and drained the last of the water from his hat. He put it on and felt a few cool drops run down his forehead.

"Howdy," Calhoun said to the Shoshoni. "It's nice to see you're feeling better."

"Thank you,' Badger Woman said.

The gambler dropped the wood and faced the Trailsman. "Are you fixing to spend the night here? If so, what are we going to do with all the bodies? I don't much like the notion of being surrounded by corpses while I sleep."

Fargo squinted up at the late afternoon sun. It would take over a day to plant so many dead under the ground, and he couldn't afford the delay. The best bet would be to let the buzzards enjoy a feast and light out to find a sheltered spot to camp for the night. He had a plan in mind, and he had to be ready by midnight. "We'll keep going and find a place to make camp," he announced.

Calhoun stared at the pile of kindling. "I sure am glad I went to all that trouble collecting wood," he muttered.

"It was good practice for later," Fargo said, and looked at the woman. "We can't take the time to bury all the dead. I'm sorry."

Badger Woman gazed at the mutilated corpses and frowned. "Leave me here. I do not want my father and mother to fill a coyote's belly. I will bury them."

The hurt in her eyes changed Fargo's mind to a degree. "Tell you what. We'll bury your immediate family, but that's it. Then you're coming with us. I'm not leaving you alone when a grizzly or a cougar might smell all this blood and follow its nose here. And there's always a slim chance Blue Raven might send some of his men back this way." He gestured at their extra mounts. "You're coming with us and that's final."

Again Badger Woman bestowed a cryptic smile on the big man. "As you wish, kind one," she said meekly.

"Kind one?" Calhoun repeated, and smirked at Fargo. "You?"

"Would you care to help me dig or get kindling?"

"I'll help dig," Calhoun said quickly.

"Though you might," Fargo said and went to work finding a suitable level plot west of the ruined village. Working with a tomahawk he found lying beside a slain warrior, he started digging shallow graves. The gambler found the bottom half of a broken spear and pitched in to help.

The Shoshoni woman came over to observe. After two graves were completed, she remarked, "My two sisters must also be buried."

So Fargo kept working until four graves were done. He tossed the tomahawk down and had Badger Woman lead him to her kin. Her father had been shot twice in the head. Her mother and both sisters had been raped and gutted. It took all of his self-control to drag the dead women to the graves without becoming sick. Calhoun helped, gagging the whole time.

The sun was an hour above the horizon when the last handfuls of dirt were thrown on top of the bodies. Fargo bowed his head and folded his hands, thinking that Badger Woman would want to say a few words commending her family to the Great Mystery. Instead, stifling tears and sniffling, she went to one of the horses and mounted.

Fargo climbed on the Ovaro and led the way to the northeast, tracking the renegades. The shallow impressions of the many hoof prints and the short strides taken by the renegades' animals indicated the band had not been in any hurry when they departed. And why should they be? As far as Blue Raven knew, there was no one else within miles.

The renegades had crossed the plain, then skirted a mountain and entered a long, serpentine valley watered by a creek. Five miles later the valley ended below a narrow pass between two lofty summits. At the base of the incline leading to the pass was a sparkling pond where the renegades had watered their animals.

Fargo halted at the pond. Reading the tracks, he knew Blue Raven had gone on through the pass. Perfect. He glanced at the others and declared, "This is where we'll camp."

"Is it safe to build a fire?" Calhoun asked.

"A small one," Fargo said, alighting. There was no way anyone on the far side of the pass could spot the flames, and the wind was blowing from the northwest, which meant the smoke would be carried into the valley. He noticed the Shoshoni woman was staring at him again, as she had done repeatedly since leaving the village.

Calhoun climbed down. "I'll get the fire going."

"And I'll hunt our supper," Fargo volunteered. He bent down to retrieve the throwing knife from his right boot, then ventured into the adjacent forest. There were plenty of birds—sparrows and chickadees and jays—and a couple of rabbits bounded from his path before he could throw. Pausing, he scoured a thicket to his left and heard a twig snap behind him.

Fargo spun, surprised to discover Badger Woman had followed him. She'd reclaimed her knife at the village and now held the weapon in her right hand. For a moment he thought she might be about to attack him. Then she smiled and stepped boldly forward until her jutting breasts were nearly touching his chest.

"I am good hunter," she whispered. "I help."

"There's no need—" Fargo began and received an impulsive kiss on the mouth that cut off his statement. He gazed into her eyes, knowing what she had in mind and curious as to why. Was she that grateful for the little he'd done? Or was there a deeper reason?

Badger Woman grinned, then pressed her shapely form flush with his. She kissed him again, her soft lips molding his own, her tongue flicking out to stroke his. Her breasts and hips ground against his body. Suddenly she drew back, beaming. "Later," she said huskily, and dashed into the undergrowth in search of game.

Fargo swallowed, feeling a lump in his throat. His skin was warm all over. The brief contact had aroused his manhood, stirring his lust to a red-hot pitch, and he no longer cared why she wanted him. He now craved her more than he did food, and he was eager for night to fall.

9

"You don't have much of an appetite," Calhoun remarked, his mouth full of the rabbit stew Badger Woman had prepared for them.

Fargo absently hefted the crude bark bowl the Shoshoni had made, drinking in her curvaceous figure with his eyes as she ate a few feet to his right. "I reckon I don't much care for food at the moment," he replied.

"Too bad," Calhoun said, chewing hungrily. "This is the best stew I've ever eaten."

Badger Woman smiled at the gambler but her gaze remained on the Trailsman.

Overhead, stars had sprouted, sparkling like fireflies. Fargo stared at the rising moon, calculating he had plenty of time to satisfy his true appetite before he had to leave. He placed the stew on the ground and said as casually as possible, "I'm going to stretch my legs."

"Not me," Calhoun said. "I plan to eat a third helping of this rabbit. Maybe a fourth."

"You need good food in you to regain your strength," Fargo said rising. He ambled toward the shimmering pond, seeing the pale reflection of the moon on its glassy surface. Bordering the east side was a narrow grassy strip ringed by dark woods. Deep shadows shrouded the base of the trees.

He strolled along the east bank until he was thirty yards from the fire. Then he moved to the edge of the trees and crouched. Calhoun and Badger Woman were still seated by the fire. The Shoshoni woman spoke to the gambler, stood, and came slowly in his direction.

Fargo focused on her swaying hips and watched her raven tresses move with the breeze. She was looking all around but hadn't spotted him yet. Grinning, he let her draw nearer until she was only two yards from where he waited. She stopped and faced the pond, searching the night for him and at that moment he moved, gliding up behind her and reaching around from the rear to cup her full breasts and kiss her on the neck.

"Ahhhhh," Badger Woman breathed, grinding her buttocks against his organ. She tilted her face so he could touch his lips to hers.

Stark lust coursed through Fargo, setting his body aflame. He didn't know whether it was the circumstances, the fact she wanted him, or the air of mystery about her, but he craved her as he had few other women. Her silky tongue met his own, stoking his inner fires, and he played his hands up and down her body. She groaned when he kneaded her thighs and touched her mound.

Fargo turned her to face him. He rammed his hardness against her mound, letting her feel how much he wanted her. She cooed softly and let her hand drop, her fingers lightly tracing the length of his erection.

He gripped her shoulders and pulled her to the base of the trees. Probing his tongue into her mouth, he sank to his knees in the grass. She slid down with him, breathing heavily through her nose. His right hand strayed to the hem of her buckskin dress and snaked under and up. The heat generated by her thighs made his palm sweat. He caressed them over and over, listening to her pant as he licked her neck. Then, without warning, he swept his hand to the triangle of hair at the juncture of her shapely legs. His middle finger slipped into her moist crack.

"Ohhhhhh," Badger Woman moaned quietly, arching her spine. She found his left ear and greedily chewed it with passionate nibbles.

Fargo teased her, letting his finger slide into her womanhood part of the way, then withdrawing it. She trembled and sucked on his ear lobe. His organ strained against his pants, eager for release. Instead, he jabbed his finger into her hot hole, causing her to stiffen and utter a low whine.

"Yes, kind one," she whispered. "Oh, yes! Do not stop."

He pumped his finger in and out, feeling her wet inner walls clamp around it. Her hips bucked and she tenderly kissed his throat. His left arm around her slim waist, he lowered her to the dank earth, then lifted the bottom of her dress, exposing her legs. He inched his left hand upward until he found her pliant breasts. Both nipples were hard and erect. Tweaking them elicited another groan and she squirmed under him.

"Do me!" she said breathlessly in his ear. "Do me, Skye Fargo."

But he wasn't ready to end it yet. He raised her dress until her globes popped free, then applied his lips to each nipple. She gasped and gripped his buttocks. For a minute he dawdled, his tongue flicking over her heaving bosom, then he knelt between her legs and trailed his tongue down her body until he came to her mound.

Badger Woman parted her legs wider, knowing what was coming next.

Fargo nuzzled into her nether lips, stabbing into her with his tongue. Her thighs clamped to the sides of his head and she gripped his hair with her hands. A tantalizing fragrance filled his nostrils, fueling his hunger for her. He kissed and licked and nibbled until her hips were bucking and she tugged on his head, pulling him up.

"Please," she said. "Oh, please."

He rose high enough to unfasten his pants, then held his shaft and aligned himself with her pulsating hole. In an instant the deed was done; he buried his organ to the hilt and saw her eyes widen and her mouth slacken as her own desire was fulfilled. He started an instinctive stroking motion, letting the friction build slowly, wanting to savor their lovemaking.

"Make me come," Badger Woman urged in a whisper.

Fargo did his best to accommodate her. He increased his rhythm, feeling her thrust her hips to meet him, his entire body tingling with sexual energy. On and on he went, devoting his mouth to her cherry red lips and her quivering breasts, the explosion building at the base of his manhood. And then, when they were both panting and pounding in furious passion, he squirted into her at the selfsame moment she came with a fluttering groan.

Badger Woman clasped him to her with all her might, her hips locked to his, riding out the culmination of their mutual ecstasy. She breathed in his ear and uttered soft words in Shoshone.

At last Fargo slowed, his own breath rasping from his

lungs, his body caked with sweat. He lay on top of her and kissed her brow, marveling at the intensity of their union. And he still didn't have any idea why she had wanted him so badly. A second later though, he received a clue.

Smiling contentedly, Badger Woman ran her fingers through his hair and gazed happily up at the twinkling heavens. "I am alive," she said softly, then repeated it a shade louder. "I am alive!"

Fargo noticed a slight smirk on Wes Calhoun's face when they finally drifted back to the fire. The gambler glanced up at them and had the tact to compose himself before speaking.

"So there you two are. I was beginning to think a grizzly ate you."

Badger Woman chuckled.

Taking a seat near Calhoun, Fargo cleared his throat and announced, "I'll be riding out in a while."

"Alone?" Calhoun asked.

Fargo nodded and fed a branch to the fire. "I'd be obliged if you would stay here and keep an eye on Badger Woman until I get back."

"How long will you be gone?"

"Depends," Fargo said, and pointed at the forest to the east of the pond. "It might be wise for you to make your camp in there, where no one can see you. Keep your fire low, your gun handy, and your eyes peeled."

Calhoun leaned forward. "Are you fixing to tangle with Blue Raven and his bunch all by yourself?"

"I am to try and get the Chambers woman out," Skye admitted.

The gambler nodded. "I thought so. Then I'm coming along. You'll need all the help you can get."

Fargo had expected his newfound friend to object and already had his argument prepared. "Wes, I appreciate the offer. But this is the kind of job for one man. I have a better chance of pulling it off alone." He paused. "Besides, you're still not fully recovered. And we sure as hell can't leave Badger Woman here alone."

"I don't know," Calhoun said. "I'm not partial to sitting

on my rump while you're out there risking your life. Especially since I owe you.''

"It can't be helped," Fargo said. "You know I'm right."

With evident reluctance Calhoun slumped and stated, "I reckon so."

Few words were spoken for the next hour. Fargo tried to make small talk, but Calhoun was in a moody funk over the state of affairs and answered with monosyllables. Badger Woman, meanwhile, sat near the flames, her knees drawn to her chest and her arms looped around her legs, a dreamy expression etching her features.

Fargo stood when he decided the time was right and walked to the Ovaro. "Take care," he said. "And stay alert." He swung into the saddle and found both of them gazing at him.

"May the Great Medicine guide your footsteps," Badger Woman said.

"Try not to get shot," Calhoun added, mustering a lopsided smile. "I'll need you around if I bump into more grizzlies."

With a wave Fargo wheeled the big stallion and rode up the incline to the pass. The moon afforded adequate illumination except in the pass proper, where the black shadows cast by the twin mountains on either hand gave him the illusion of entering a cave. He rode slowly, his right hand on the Colt, the dull thud of the pinto's feet echoing faintly off the twin summits.

Now he couldn't afford to let down his guard for a second. Somewhere out there was a murdering butcher who would slay him on sight. He was counting on the element of surprirse to work in his favor. Since Blue Raven had no idea someone was pursuing the band, the renegades probably had a fire going. And at night a campfire would be easy to spot from a considerable distance off.

Skye tensed as he neared the opposite end of the pass. There was always the possibility that Blue Raven had camped not far beyond, in which case there might be a guard or two posted at the pass as a simple precaution. But he came to the end without incident, and before him lay a long valley, a sea of dark foliage extending for miles.

He spied the flickering light a second later and grinned.

Perhaps two miles off was a campfire, situated near the base of the mountain bordering the valley on the west. The light served as a beacon, drawing him unerringly to the men he sought. He rode as fast as he dared for the first mile, then cautiously slowed and neared the site at a walk.

When he was still over a hundred yards off, he heard gruff laughter and cheerful voices. The renegades were having a good time. He dismounted, tied the reins to a tree limb, then pulled the Sharps from its case. The rifle firmly in hand, he advanced with all the stealth at his command, planting each boot with consummate care, wary of a twig breaking underfoot.

The voices became more distinct. Some of the renegades were speaking in the Sioux tongue, others English. The gist of the conversations revolved around the attack on the Shoshoni village, with each renegade boasting of his exploits. He heard one man brag about cutting off a woman's breasts so the skin could be used to make a tobacco pouch. Another mentioned how he had raped four of the women.

Twenty-five yards from the band Fargo halted behind a tree and scrutinized the lay of the land ahead. Blue Raven had picked the site well. The renegades were in a spacious clearing fringed by woods and backed by the mountain. Their large fire revealed everything. Seated in several groups, many were drinking liquor. He counted twelve men, just as Badger Woman had said. Eight were half-breeds, two were Sioux, and two were Cheyennes. All outcasts, all seasoned killers. Their horses and the animals that had been stolen were tethered to the north.

Fargo scanned the hard faces and spotted Blue Raven. The killer sat about eight feet from the fire with his back to the mountain, easy to identify because of his beaver hat, Army coat, and red scarf. Blue Raven possessed a stocky build, a fleshy face, and an oversized hooked nose that lent him the aspect of a bird of prey. Four other renegades were sitting in front of him.

But where was the woman?

Alarmed, Fargo surveyed the camp again and didn't see her. Had the renegades already had their fun and murdered the poor woman? Keeping bent at the waist, he moved to

75

the left, going from pine tree to pine tree. Suddenly he drew up short. Lying directly behind Blue Raven was a sizable brown bundlle that had moved slightly. He studied it and realized that the bundle was a person; Susan Chambers curled up in a fetal position, a rope around her neck with the end in Blue Raven's lap.

Fargo was keenly tempted to shoot the renegade chief right then and there. But if he did, the rest would be after him in a flash. He'd never be able to get the woman out. Dropping to his elbows and knees, he began crawling closer. The undergrowth screened him from the renegades, enabling him to reach a spot ten feet from the clearing. In the shelter of a thick, squat bush he halted and peeked out.

Two of the band were preparing their bedding. Fargo hoped most of the others would soon follow suit. Somehow, he must sneak in there and get Chambers out, and the chore would be a hair less hazardous if most of the renegades were in dreamland.

Unexpectedly, one of the half-breeds stood and walked directly toward the spot where Fargo lay concealed. He froze, wondering if he'd been detected, and saw several others look in his direction. Cocking the rifle, he braced for the worst.

10

Fargo heard the half-breed speak in the Sioux tongue, a language with which he was somewhat familiar.

"I will get more wood. Then I'll finish the story."

Of all the luck! Fargo pressed himself flat, intently watching the half-breed, dreading the consequences of an outcry. The man wore only buckskin pants and moccasins. Strapped around his waist were a Dragoon and a butcher knife. Fargo touched his finger to the trigger, ready to rise up and cut loose if need be.

The renegade slanted to the west six or seven feet and stopped near a tree. He started picking up busted sections of limbs for the fire, moving from side to side as he searched.

Fargo held himself still, certain he would be discovered. But the half-breed turned to the west and found a number of branches that suited his purpose. Scooping them up, the renegade promptly hastened back to his companions. Fargo realized he had been holding his breath and released it. Talk about close shaves. He gazed at Susan Chambers, racking his brain for a way to get her out of that nest of vipers alive.

He noticed that the base of the mountain to the rear of the camp was covered with high weeds and dotted with evergreens. About twelve feet separated Susan Chambers from the cover. Twisting, he retreated a half-dozen yards, then rose into a crouch and made for the mountain.

Four of the renegades were turning in when he reached the slope and halted behind a boulder to get his bearings. Most of the killers now had their backs to him, including Blue Raven. The woman hadn't moved and she appeared to have her face buried in her hands. Maybe she was crying. He couldn't tell.

Fargo flattened his body and crawled into a patch of waist-high weeds, using the barrel of the Sharps to carefully part the vegetation and minimize the rustling he caused. The renegades were talking loud enough to drown out any noise he made, but he wasn't taking anything for granted. He watched the tops of the weeds, making sure none waved too wildly for fear of attracting the attention of one of the killers.

As quietly as any Indian who ever lived, Fargo moved northward until he was abreast of the Chambers woman. He stopped and slid down the slope, using the available cover, until he was prone in dense weeds and could see the camp clearly. Now he had to wait.

The minutes dragged by. Seven of the renegades reclined on blankets, one hardy killer on the bare ground. Still, Blue Raven and four others chatted on.

Fargo was impatient for them to hit the sack. Intent on observing them, he didn't realize something was beside him until he heard a soft rustling noise and suddenly felt the slightest of pressure on his lower legs. His instinctive reaction was to turn and see what it was, but as he began to swivel his neck he heard another sound—a sound that chilled the blood in his veins—the brief yet distinct and unmistakable buzzing of a rattlesnake's tail.

He stiffened, freezing in place, and felt the snake pause on top of him. His skin crawled at the idea of having one of the deadly reptiles perched on his body, but there was nothing he could do. If he tried to grab it, the rattler might bite. If he tried rolling to either side, not only might the snake strike but the renegades were certain to spot the commotion in the weeds and rush to investigate. Even attempting to ease his legs out from under the rattlesnake could provoke an attack.

Fargo imitated a rock and waited for the snake to leave. He knew most rattlers did their hunting at night, preferring to lie up in the heat of the day or to sun themselves on rocks. The snake must have been on its nocturnal rounds and simply stumbled on him. Would it bite if he didn't move? That was the crucial question.

He tried to recollect all the accounts he'd heard of rattlesnake attacks. Most, as he recalled, had taken place during daylight hours when a man or a horse stepped on one sunning itself. A few men, though, had been bitten while out walking at night after blundering onto a rattler. In most cases the snake had been startled or otherwise agitated. Maybe, if he did nothing, the reptile would depart.

At least a minute elapsed and the rattlesnake didn't budge.

Fargo broke out in a cold sweat. He breathed shallowly, concerned the least little movement would result in the rattler burying its fangs in his flesh. An irritating itch developed at the small of his back, growing worse by the second. Gritting his teeth, he endured the discomfort.

Two more of the renegades lay down.

Suddenly the reptile moved. Fargo could feel its scales sliding across his buckskins and heard the snake slip into the weeds on his right. The pressure on his legs disappeared and he glanced around in time to see the rattler's tail vanish in the vegetation. An involuntary shiver rippled down his body and he sighed in relief.

Back to business, Skye reflected, concentrating on the camp again. Only Blue Raven and another renegade were still awake, talking in low tones in the Sioux language. He caught a few words now and then and gathered they were discussing the route of travel they would take the next day.

At last the two men began to spread blankets on the ground.

Fargo had noticed that Susan Chambers barely twitched the entire time. She lay in that fetal position, her hair hanging over her face, her arms held close to her body. He saw Blue Raven deposit the end of the rope on the ground as the killer prepared the blanket, then watched with interest as Blue Raven tied the rope around his left wrist.

The renegade chief addressed Chambers, who made no reply. Blue Raven cursed her, then moved closer to kick her in the back. Recoiling in agony, Susan Chambers lifted her head and cried out.

For the first time Fargo saw her face. She was caked with grime and bore several bruises. Even so, she had lovely features, with high cheekbones and full lips. His sympathy for her intensified when Blue Raven kicked her again for no apparent reason other than sheer spite. Then the renegade reclined on his back and the woman curled into a ball once more.

He scanned the camp, delighted that the renegades had failed to post a guard. And why should they? As far as Blue Raven knew, they were completely safe. They had stolen the horses of the party sent from the wagon train and undoubtedly believed they had butchered every last Shoshoni at the village. There was no one after them, no one to report the atrocity. Or so they thought.

Fargo settled down to wait until every renegade was deep in slumber. Then he would make his move. The moon rose higher, casting a pale glow over the mountains. Crickets chirped around him and in the distance a coyote yipped. The wind picked up, constantly stirring the weeds.

Many of the renegades were snoring when Fargo placed the Sharps on the ground, drew his right knee forward, and reached into his boot for the Arkansas toothpick. Gripping the hilt firmly, he slowly crawled from concealment toward the dejected figure of the woman.

Somewhere to the north an owl hooted.

Fargo never took his eyes off the sleeping killers. If just one should awaken now and spot him, they would all swarm over him before he could free Chambers. Whenever a renegade stirred, he stopped and waited for the man to resume sleeping soundly. One of the half-breeds muttered in his sleep every so often and tossed from side to side. Fargo paid particular attention to him.

Six feet from the woman Fargo could hear her sniffling. He inched closer, aware that she posed as much of a danger as her abductors. If she should inadvertently scream or make any loud noise when he reached her, there would be hell to pay.

The half-breed who was muttering a lot abruptly shifted, rolling from his side onto his back. He smacked his lips, grunted, and lay still.

Fargo crawled within a foot of the woman, listening to the fire crackle and hiss as gray smoke billowed skyward. The renegades slept on, oblivious to his presence. He inched a bit closer, then extended his left hand and gently tapped her right forearm with a finger.

Susan Chambers stopped sniffling. For a moment she was a statue, then she cautiously tilted her head, gazing around her in confusion. Her gaze swiveled to Fargo. He quickly placed a finger to his lips, ready to clamp a hand over her mouth should she open it to shout. To her credit, she only blinked in surprise. Hope blossomed in her eyes and she rose on her elbows.

Fargo motioned for her to stay still. He wagged the knife, then pointed at the rope encircling her neck to let her know what he had in mind. She nodded gamely.

Warily watching the renegades, Fargo inched closer. He slipped his fingers under the rope on the side of her slender neck and pried it loose from her skin, then inserted the slim blade of his knife and started slicing outward on the strands. She studied him all the while, her face alight with relief. He could tell that she was also terrified they would be discovered before he cut her loose.

The rope finally parted and fell to the ground. Susan Chambers went to rise, but Fargo placed a hand on her shoulder to restrain her. He double-checked the renegades, verified they were all asleep, then rose to a crouch and helped her to do the same. Gesturing, he let her go past him toward the weeds. He hastily wedged the throwing knife under his gunbelt, then placed his right hand on the .44 and backpedaled.

All was going well.

He glanced at the woman, saw she was a few feet from cover, and faced the renegades. At that moment, from the north, arose a loud whinny from one of the renegades' mounts. The half-breed doing all the muttering abruptly sat up and surveyed the camp, his eyes drooping sleepily. But the instant he saw Fargo, they widened in consternation.

Fargo knew what would happen next. He swept the Colt out as the man went to yell, and fired. The slug struck the half-breed in the forehead and slammed him backward. Whirling, Fargo reached the woman in three bounds, gripped her elbow and propelled her into the weeds. It took but a moment to retrieve the Sharps. Then he was racing to the south with Chambers at his side and looking back to see if the renegades were in pursuit.

Rampant confusion reigned in the camp. Blue Raven and his killers were on their feet, shouting, voicing questions, sluggish from the effects of their slumber, trying to ascertain where the shot came from. A few noticed the dead man. Blue

Raven saw that the woman was gone and bellowed in rage. And then a beefy renegade glanced toward the mountain and glimpsed the two fleeing forms.

"There!"

Fargo saw eleven guns swing in their direction and dived, looping his left arm around the woman's waist and bearing both of them to the ground. The night rocked with thunder and bullets buzzed overhead. Rising to his knees, Fargo discovered four of the renegades were charging in pursuit and holstered the Colt. He snapped the Sharps to his shoulder, took a hasty bead on the foremost cutthroat, and fired.

The shot hurled the man backward into his companions and the rest of the band flattened or scrambled behind saddles.

Seizing the woman's arm, Fargo hauled her off the ground and raced southward, staying low. He'd bought them a minute at the most. Then the renegades would regroup and be after them with a vengeance. The woods loomed ahead and he barreled into the undergrowth, pulling her along. Immediately he headed for the Ovaro.

In the camp a gruff voice was issuing orders. "After them, you dogs! I want the woman alive! Go! Go!"

Fargo wished he'd shot Blue Raven instead of the other renegade. Branches lashed at his face and jabbed his buckskins. He didn't bother trying to exercise stealth; speed was the important thing. If they could reach the Ovaro, the odds were good they could make it through the pass well ahead of the renegades.

Some of the band had entered the woods. They were yelling back and forth, trying to spot the woman and her rescuer.

Susan Chambers ran all out, determination lining her face. She glanced often at the big man at her side.

Reaching a small clearing, Fargo paused to check to their rear. None of the renegades appeared close enough to pose a threat. He kept going, traveling another ten yards when he detected the drumming of hooves and realized some of the butchers had wisely gone for their horses before giving chase. That meant trouble.

He increased his speed, Susan Chambers breathing heavily

as she did her best to maintain the pace. To the east a rider or two crashed through the brush, searching for them. Fargo was ready to fire but saw no one to shoot at.

Before long a vague shape materialized up ahead. Fargo recognized the stallion and grinned. He listened intently, estimating the location of the renegades. Men on foot were twenty-five yards behind them, while to the southeast the horsemen were conducting a sweep.

Suddenly Susan stumbled.

Fargo caught her in time to prevent her from falling, then held her hand as they ran the rest of the way. Hurriedly, he slipped the rifle into its case, then put the throwing knife in his boot. "We'll have to ride double," he whispered, swinging into the saddle.

"Who are you?" she asked.

"Skye Fargo, at your service, ma'am," he answered, reaching down.

"Why did you save me from those devils?"

"I'll explain once we're out of the frying pan," Fargo said. She took hold and he swung her up behind him. "Hold on tight," he advised. "And keep your head down."

Skye wheeled the Ovaro and started in the direction of the pass and safety. In the pale moonglow appearances were deceiving. Every shadow seemed alive. He strained to catch sight of the horsemen, not wanting to blunder onto one in the dark. The very next moment, however, a renegade found him. He saw the indistinct shapes of both horse and rider charging from the southeast and heard a loud shot.

"Here they are! Over here!"

Fargo drew the Colt, but the barrel was nowhere near level when the renegade fired.

11

A lead hornet whizzed past Fargo's head, and then he answered the report with a blast from the .44. His aim was more accurate. The renegade screeched and toppled from his mount. Spurring the stallion forward, Fargo raced twenty yards, then spied other horsemen approaching; one from the south, another from the southeast. He'd miscalculated how many there were.

Rather than confront them head-on and risk the life of the woman, and since the route to the pass was effectively blocked, Fargo cut to the west, intending to swing around the mountain flanking the renegade camp. As he turned, shots cracked, and Susan Chambers gasped and clung to him with all her might. He could feel her bosom mashing into his back.

There were angry shouts from the renegades on foot. Someone yelled that they should all get their horses.

Fargo pushed the pinto as hard as he dared, expertly threading among the trees and thickets, glancing back constantly to check on their pursuers. For a while the outcome was in doubt as the horsemen stayed close on his heels, then gradually the Ovaro began to gain ground. He reached the south side of the mountain and galloped along its base to the west.

To the rear, the renegade camp was in an uproar as the butchers hastily saddled their mounts, many cursing loudly, their horses neighing nervously in all the confusion.

Fargo looked back to see the pair of renegades still after him, perhaps thirty yards behind. They were holding their fire because of the intervening vegetation. If he could lose them, he stood a good chance of escaping free and clear. If he didn't, they would guide the rest to his location.

Suddenly the trees ended and a flat stretch of hard ground dotted with boulders appeared. Some were bigger than the stallion, and he wound among them to confuse the renegades on his trail.

One of the killers shouted in the Sioux tongue, "This direction! Come this way!"

Leading on the others, Fargo thought with a scowl. A particularly huge boulder loomed on his left, and on an impulse he rode behind it, spun the stallion, and halted. He cocked the Colt, hearing the pounding hooves and the pursuers' mounts grow steadily louder and louder. Then both men were right there, riding side by side not six feet away.

Fargo snapped off a shot that struck the nearest rider in the head. The man slumped over his saddle, exposing the second renegade who twisted and tried to bring a rifle to bear. Fargo shot him twice, and the renegade's arms were flung outward as the man fell.

Sliding the .44 into its holster, Fargo tightened his grip on the reins and resumed his desperate bid to rescue the woman. By his reckoning there were eight renegades remaining, eight savage killers who would be incensed at the deaths of their fellows and would stop at nothing to get revenge. And since Blue Raven was known for being tenacious as well as bloodthirsty, he knew the band would never give up of its own accord. He must think of a way to lose them or discourage them.

Giving the band the slip might be next to impossible. They were bound to be competent trackers, and one or two might even qualify as his equals in that regard. His best bet was to reduce their numbers even further, to convince them the cost of trying to recapture the woman was too high.

In another mile the terrain changed again, becoming a narrow strip of dense woodland between the mountain on his right and another mountain on the left. He entered the gap because he had no choice, although he disliked being hemmed in. "Are you all right, ma'am?" he thought to ask, realizing the woman had not said a word since the chase began.

"Fine," was her muffled reply. "And please call me Susan."

"If our luck holds we'll shake these hombres before too long," Fargo assured her.

"I hope so. I'd rather die than be in their clutches again.

They did things to me," Susan said, her voice quivering. She added in a horrified tone, "Terrible things."

"Don't talk about it," Fargo advised. "Don't even think about it."

"Easier said than done," she replied forlornly.

Anger seized Fargo. So the sons of bitches had abused her! He thought of the poor Shoshonis, the men cut down mercilessly, the women raped and mutilated, and all of them left to rot. He thought of all the other innocent folks who had lost their lives or been brutalized by the band over the years, and a steely resolve to pay Blue Raven and his bunch back for their atrocities welled up within him.

Fargo noticed that the gap between the moutains had narrowed, and sheer rock walls reared on both sides. The trees thinned out, the soil too hard and arid to support plant life. The Ovaro's hooves struck the earth underfoot like hammers striking stone, the sounds amplified by the walls. He craned his neck to peer up at the rims.

"Mind telling me why you saved my life now?" Susan asked softly.

"You needed saving," Fargo said. Since he couldn't hear any sound of pursuit, he figured they had a comfortable lead on the renegades. For the time being, anyway. There was no need to discourage her from talking. It might make her feel better.

"But how did you know they had abducted me?"

"A man named Seth Purdy told me," Fargo said and briefly related the sequence of events leading to his appearance at the renegade camp.

"Mr. Purdy and his son were decent people," Susan commented sadly when he was through. "So were the others. And they all died because of me."

"You can't hardly blame yourself for what happened. Blue Raven is responsible, not you."

"If I hadn't stepped out of our wagon to see what all the shooting was about, Blue Raven would never have taken me," Susan said, her tone laden with guilt. "I should have listened to my pa. He's dead because of me, too."

"Your pa is still alive," Fargo corrected her and heard her sharp intake of breath.

"I saw him get shot."

"He was hit, but he's hanging on," Fargo disclosed. "They're taking real good care of him, and he should be on his feet in a month."

"Thank God," Susan breathed.

They came to a bend in the ravine and Fargo found himself riding northward. A disturbing thought occurred to him. What if the ravine was a dead end? They would be boxed in, at Blue Raven's mercy. He began eagerly seeking a means out, scouring the walls and the ground ahead.

"Not many men would do what you've done," Susan remarked. "You could have been killed."

"We both still may be," Fargo mentioned. "We're not out of the woods yet by a long shot." He felt her tense at the reminder. She tightened her grip around his waist and rested a cheek between his shoulder blades.

Soon, to Fargo's relief, they found the end of the ravine. Before them was an expanse of woodland stretching several miles to another mountain. He rode on, losing all track of time as the minutes dragged out into an hour, then two. The moon started on its downward course.

Twice Fargo came upon low hills and rode to the top to scan his backtrail. Neither time did he spot or hear the renegades. It bothered him. There should have been some sign of the killers by now, he reflected, unless, by some miracle, Blue Raven had given up the chase.

When still a mile from the mountain Fargo came on a grassy meadow with a shallow stream in the center. He reined up at the water's edge so the stallion could drink, then looked over his shoulder at the Chambers woman. "You can get down and stretch your legs," he said.

Lifting her head, Susan gazed listlessly at the countryside, then slid to the ground. She crossed her arms and stood with her slim shoulders slumped, the perfect picture of abject depression.

"Something wrong?" Fargo asked, climbing down.

She uttered a bitter laugh. "What could possibly be wrong? My whole life is ruined, is all."

"How do you figure?"

Susan glanced at him. "Do I need to go into every sordid

detail? Those vermin had their way with me. They took turns pawing and poking and doing things only a sweetheart or a husband should do. No decent man will want me after this."

Fargo saw her eyes moisten, then she looked away. He frowned, realizing here was a modest, almost prim woman who had regarded her sexual purity as some sort of prize for the right man to win—a woman from a proper family who had been taught to keep her legs crossed until then. And now she believed she had been spoiled, tarnished beyond redemption by the renegades. "You're wrong," he said. "Any decent man would be proud to call you his woman."

"You're just saying that to cheer me up."

"Like hell I am," Fargo said. "You're not wearing a brand on your forehead, are you? No one will ever know what happened to you unless you tell them, and there's no need to do that."

"But isn't that dishonest? If I meet a man who is interested in me, don't I owe it to him to tell him?"

"Why? It's done and over with. Put it behind you and get on with your life. The kind of man you're looking for will be more interested in you as a person, not the number of times you've been poked."

Susan pondered his comments for a minute, her forehead furrowed in deep contemplation. Finally she looked into his eyes and bluntly asked, "Would you go to bed with me, knowing what you know?"

Fargo stared at her—at her luxurious blond hair and full figure, at the swell of her breasts and the contours of her legs—and felt faint stirrings below his belt. "Of course. Any man would. It's only natural."

"It wouldn't make you feel dirty?"

"Not unless we did it in a mud hole," Fargo said, and smiled when she burst into hearty laughter. For a moment all her cares dissipated and she radiated a sensual beauty. Then he heard a raucous cry to the south, the screech of a jay, and turned.

Susan instantly stopped laughing. "What is it?"

"Blue Raven, I reckon."

"How do you know?"

"Did you hear the jay?"

"Yes. So?"

"So jays aren't night birds. They hole up in trees after dark to rest. And they only cry out like that when they're spooked," Fargo explained.

"Maybe an animal was after it," Susan suggested.

"Maybe," Fargo said. But he wasn't taking any chances. He quickly mounted and helped her up behind him, then crossed the stream and rode hard toward the mountain. He was almost to the far side of the meadow when she spoke up.

"I see something behind us."

Fargo shifted and looked. Sure enough, he made out the indistinct outline of a horse and rider a second before the pounding of the animal's hooves announced its presence. He brought the Ovaro to a gallop, plunging into the forest as a savage shriek erupted.

"It's one of them!" Susan cried.

He already knew that. But why only one? Where were the rest? Then he heard the crack of a gun; once, twice, three times in swift succession, and knew the renegade had signaled the others. Now he understood. The renegades had lost the trail or found it too difficult to follow rapidly at night. Blue Raven had sent one of his men on ahead, probably on the best horse, with orders to try and overtake them and fire shots when he caught up. The renegades would ride to the sound of the shots and not have to bother with time-consuming tracking. Clever of the bastard, Skye mused.

The stallion ably avoided the trees in their path as they raced deeper into the forest. Fargo saw a low limb ahead and called out, "Duck!" He hunched down, the branch narrowly missing his hat. Straightening, he spied a dimly illuminated clearing twenty yards ahead and the sight gave him an idea. He needed to dispose of the renegade on their heels before Blue Raven and the rest of the band caught up, and he needed to do it quietly. A gunshot would help the band find them that much sooner.

At the clearing Fargo halted. "I want you to sit in the saddle and don't budge," he said, easing down, being careful not to bump her with his leg.

"What are you going to do?" Susan asked nervously.

"Use you as bait," Fargo said. "Are you willing?"

Susan blinked, then gulped, and nodded. ''Whatever you need. I trust you, Skye.''

''Just look pretty,'' Fargo directed with a grin and a wink, and moved toward the trees. He recalled Blue Raven telling the renegades to take her alive, and he was counting on that for his plan to succeed. From the tree line issued loud crackling as their pursuer plunged into the undergrowth. He went several feet into the woods, halted behind a pine, and palmed the throwing knife.

Susan Chambers slid onto the saddle and held the reins in her right hand. She turned the Ovaro so she was facing toward the oncoming renegade, her head held high, her lips compressed.

Fargo crouched, gripped the hilt firmly, and waited. He scanned their backtrail, ready to move if the renegade came at them from a slightly different direction. The man was relying on sight and probably wouldn't follow exactly in their footsteps. A flicker of movement to the north proved him right. He glimpsed the renegade riding between two trees, and the line of travel indicated the man would pass him by five yards on his left. Staying low, he darted in that direction and squatted beside a thick waist-high bush. With any luck the renegade would concentrate on Susan and never see him.

The man abruptly slowed, his gaze on the blond woman. In his right hand was a rifle.

Fargo could see the rider's face. The man looked around suspiciously, obviously suspecting a trick. But he didn't look down, and moments later he was almost to Fargo's position. Coiling his legs, Fargo waited until the horse was a yard away, then leaped, his arms outstretched.

At the same instant the rider turned his mount toward Susan Chambers.

Caught off-guard, Fargo collided with the animal's shoulder. The impact knocked him onto his back, unharmed but fully exposed, and he glanced up to find the renegade training the rifle on his chest.

12

Fargo reacted without conscious thought. His right hand streaked up and in, hurling the throwing knife in the same manner he had countless times before. The razor tip struck the renegade at the base of the neck, the blade sliding all the way in to the hilt.

Recoiling in shock, the renegade dropped his rifle and grabbed at the protruding hilt so he could wrench the knife free. As he did, a crimson geyser sprayed out.

Fargo glimpsed all this as he rolled to the left, rising into a crouch with the .44 sweeping clear. He held his fire, watching the man, a half-breed, sputter and wheeze. His knife fell from the man's slick fingers.

Whining pitiably, the renegade tried to goad his mount forward but was too weak. He swayed to the right, then the left, his hands pressed to his ravaged throat in a vain attempt to stem the flow of precious fluid. His terrified gaze fell on the big man in buckskins and he glowered. Suddenly, his spine arching, he gasped and toppled off the right side of his animal.

Fargo walked around the horse to verify that the half-breed was indeed dead. All it took was one look at the man's slack mouth, wide eyes, and limp extended limbs to confirm the knife had done the job. Holstering the Colt, he found the toothpick and the rifle. He wiped the blade clean on the grass, replaced it in the boot sheath, and took hold of the brown stallion's reins.

Susan Chambers was exactly where he had left her, a peculiar look in her eyes as he approached. "You're very good," she said.

Was she mocking him? Fargo wondered. He shrugged and lifted the reins. "Now you have a horse of your own. Are you up to riding?"

"Just watch me," Susan said, climbing down from the Ovaro and stepping to the half-breed's animal. She took the reins and swung up, her dress hitching high enough to expose a smooth thigh before she straightened.

Smiling at her enthusiasm, Fargo slid the renegade's rifle into the holster on the man's horse and then mounted the pinto. He gazed at the body and said, "Seven left."

"I hope you kill every one of them," Susan said bitterly.

Turning the pinto, Fargo resumed their flight. Every minute was taking them farther from Calhoun and Badger Woman, which he didn't like. But he wasn't about to lead the band in the direction of his friends. As the minutes passed one into another, he speculated on how he might further reduce the odds should the rest of the renegades catch up.

The moon was near the western horizon when Fargo happened to glance at Susan and saw her eyes drooping. He chided himself for being a fool. After all she had been through, she must be exhausted. Not once had she complained, though; she had more courage than she gave herself credit for. He surveyed the landscape ahead, seeking a place to lay up for a while.

They were in the middle of a wide valley, with high grass all around them. A few hundred yards to the northeast lay a flat-topped hill, its slopes sparsely covered with brush and trees.

Fargo liked the looks of it. From the top he would be able to see for miles and spot the renegades a long way off. "How about if we stop for a spell?" he recommended.

Susan stared at him. "Is it safe?"

"Our horses could use the rest," Fargo tactfully observed.

"Oh," Susan said, as if the idea had never occurred to her. She started to yawn, then quickly covered her mouth. Rather self-consciously, she lowered her hand. "Sorry. Guess I'm a little tired."

"All the more reason to take a break," Fargo said. He pointed at the hill. "There's where we'll rest for a while," he told her and angled toward it.

Susan stayed by his side. "Not too long, I hope."

"No longer than necessary."

At the summit Fargo found plenty of grass for the horses. He ground-hitched both and joined Susan at the south rim where they had a clear view of their backtrail. She looked at him as he took a seat.

"Are you married, Skye?"

"No," Fargo said. "I'm not about to get hitched any time soon. I like to roam too much to let any woman tie me down."

"I bet a man like you has had his share of ladies," Susan said with a playful twinkle in her eyes.

"I reckon," Fargo answered, wondering what she was getting at. "Now why don't you lie down for a while? We'll be leaving before you know it."

"All right," Susan said and gazed at the ground around them. "I wish I had a pillow."

Fargo tapped his thigh. "Use my leg if you want," he offered.

Susan stared at him for a moment, thinking deeply, then bobbed her chin. "Why not?" she said and scooted closer so she could recline on her right side with her cheek in his lap. "My, your legs are warm," she remarked.

"From all the riding we've done," Fargo said and felt his skin grow warmer under her head. He forced himself not to dwell on her striking physical charms. She was counting on him to get her safely back to the wagon train, not to take advantage of her fragile emotional state.

He looked down at her and saw her eyes were already closed, a faint smile curling her lips. A good sign, he thought. The sooner she learned to laugh and grin again, the sooner she'd recover from her ordeal. Leaning on his left hand, he idly scanned their backtrail and pondered his next move.

From the top of the hill he could see over a thousand yards to the tract of forested land bordering the valley. The terrain was essentially level, and there was nowhere an enemy could hide other than in the tall grass. The sight prompted an idea.

Fargo studied the valley with renewed interest. Once dawn broke he would be able to see much better, and from his vantage point he might be able to reduce the odds greatly with the Sharps. Thanks to the rifle's extended range, he could do so without fear of Susan being harmed. If he killed Blue Raven and one or two of the other renegades, the rest might well turn tail and head for parts unknown.

The more he thought of it, the more Fargo liked the plan. He glanced at the moon, well on its way to bidding the cool night good-bye, then at the shadowy forest. The renegades hadn't appeared yet, but they would eventually. He could feel it in his bones. And they would probably be riding hard after finding their dead friend, which would make them careless.

He heard a soft, fluttering sound and glanced down at Susan Chambers. She was asleep and snoring lightly—perhaps the first real sleep she'd enjoyed since being abducted from the wagon train. He wished they could stay there indefinitely so she could catch up on her rest.

A pale glow rimmed the eastern horizon even as the moon relinquished its celestial berth. The sky gradually brightened and the fiery tip of the sun rose, attended by the chirping and singing of countless birds.

Fargo let Susan sleep in peace. He scanned the tree line repeatedly and was rewarded for his patience by spotting the first three riders when they abruptly appeared. Tensing, he gently lifted Susan's head and slid his leg out from under her, then lowered her cheek to the grass. She mumbled but didn't awaken.

Rising, the big man hurried to his stallion and yanked the Sharps from its casing. He returned to the crest and took up a position beside the slumbering woman. Dropping to his left knee, he fed a round into the chamber, then peered down the barrel at the advancing renegades, estimating distance and figuring the elevation. He lowered the rifle and adjusted the sights to his satisfaction.

Susan stirred, smacking her rosy lips loudly a few times and rolling onto her back.

There was nothing for Fargo to do but wait. He intended to try a long shot by any standards; approximately five hundred yards. If he tried any sooner, he increased the likelihood of missing. If he let the band get closer than that, there wouldn't be enough time to make a getaway should they mount a concerted charge.

He squinted, studying the killers. To his annoyance, Blue Raven wasn't in the lead. An Indian appeared to be—either one of the outcast Sioux or Cheyennes—engrossed in tracking. Then came another renegade, then Blue Raven and the rest in a tight cluster. Seven, just as he'd calculated.

Slowly the renegades drew nearer. From the way their horses were walking, Fargo knew the animals were tired. Blue Raven probably hadn't stopped once to rest since the chase commenced, which meant the Ovaro and the other stallion would be a bit fresher when the pursuit resumed. He checked the sights again, anxious to fire, and reined in his impatience.

The butchers were now eight hundred yards off.

Fargo leaned to his left and gave Susan's shoulder a mild shake. When she failed to respond, he shook her again, only harder.

Inhaling deeply, Susan opened her eyes and instantly sat up, fear contorting her face. She glanced wildly around, then saw Skye. For a few seconds she gazed at him in confusion, as if she had no idea who he was.

"Susan?" Fargo said, counting on the sound of his voice to bring her around.

"Oh. Skye," she said tentatively, then placed a palm on her forehead. "Now I remember. Thank God. I dreamt I was still in Blue Raven's hands."

"Speak of the devil," Fargo said, and nodded.

Susan looked and stiffened. "It's them!" she blurted. "Why didn't you wake me sooner? We should be miles from here."

"Calm down. We're not running just yet."

Her gaze fell on the Sharps. "What do you have in mind?"

"I aim to cut down the odds a mite."

"Is there anything I can do?"

"Mount up and hold my stallion's reins for me. We may need to light out in a hurry."

Grinning, Susan rose, bending over so her silhouette wouldn't be seen by the renegades and hastened to the horses. She climbed on her mount and bent down to take the Ovaro's reins in her left hand.

Fargo turned his attention to the renegades. He aligned the rifle stock against his right shoulder and thumbed back the hammer. The band was still seven hundred yards off. Too far. He sighted on them anyway, working out in his mind the number of inches he must raise the barrel when he fired to guarantee the proper trajectory.

Blue Raven unexpectedly moved his horse up alongside the Indian doing the tracking. They conversed, with the tracker gesturing several times at the ground.

Were they discussing how far behind they were? Fargo wondered. He saw Blue Raven lift the beaver hat and mop at his brow. With any luck he would plant a slug in that hat in another minute or two.

A third of the blazing sun was now above the eastern horizon, lending a golden haze to the air over the secluded valley.

Six hundred yards separated the renegades from the hill. Fargo sighted on Blue Raven and held the heavy rifle steady. Not yet, he had to remind himself. His trigger finger tingled. A cramp flared in his left leg but he ignored it.

Susan's mount chose that moment to whinny.

Fargo tensed, dreading the renegades had heard. They came on, though, apparently unaware of the noise. Still holding Blue Raven in his sights, he noted they were near the point at which he would fire. He carefully elevated the barrel, scarcely breathing, his nerves stretched taut.

The renegades reached the proper spot.

Skye saw the Indian tracker glance toward the hill a heartbeat before he squeezed the trigger. Whether the Indian somehow saw him or saw sunlight glinting off the rifle barrel, he would never know. But the very next instant, the exact instant the Trailsman fired, the tracker suddenly turned his horse in front of Blue Raven and motioned excitedly at the hill.

The renegades began to fan out.

A second later the shot hit home, the slug evidently taking the tracker squarely between the shoulder blades. The man's arms flew outward and he was knocked forward over the neck of his mount, as if by a gigantic invisible fist and tumbled in a heap in the grass.

Fargo, peeved, swiftly ejected the spent round and inserted another. The renegades were scattering to the right and left, Blue Raven shouting commands. He took a bead on the stocky figure and started to lift the barrel in compensation for the range. To his surprise, the killers dismounted, clawing their rifles from their saddles and flattened themselves in the high grass. Before he could fire again, there were no targets to hit except their horses.

Smart thinking, Fargo mused. He'd counted on their either recklessly attacking or panicking and trying to flee. Either way, he would have had time to kill two or three. He scanned the grass, speculating on whether the renegades would stay put or creep toward the hill. If he was in their boots, he sure as hell wouldn't just lie there.

He delayed leaving, hoping to spy one of the butchers. Suddenly he did; on the right a half-breed brazenly stood with a rifle pressed to his shoulder. He swung the Sharps to bag the dunderhead, thinking that any fool would know better than to match an ordinary rifle against a Sharps. Then the half-breed fired, and the exceptionally loud retort caused Fargo to pause in consternation. As one who had used a Sharps for years, he knew the distinctive sound of the big gun better than most. And damned if that wasn't a Sharps. No sooner did the realization hit home than the ball hit the rim of the hill within inches of his feet.

Fargo threw himself into a roll to the right, winding up on his stomach with the Sharps ready to fire. But the half-breed had dropped from sight again, the grass waving in his wake. The unforeseen development of confronting an enemy armed with a rifle every bit as powerful as Fargo's own cast the fight in a whole new light. He quickly scrambled backward from the crest, not bothering to rise until he had retreated over six feet and felt safe from the hidden marksman.

Susan Chambers took one look at his face as he ran to the Ovaro and asked, "What's wrong?"

"One of those bastards has a Sharps," Fargo said, sliding his rifle into its saddle case.

"So?"

Fargo swung into the saddle. "So I don't have the edge I figured I did."

"Does this mean we're in trouble?"

"Big trouble," Fargo confirmed, spurring the pinto forward, leading the way down the opposite slope and toward woodland a quarter of a mile away. Could they reach it before the renegade with the Sharps reached the top of the hill? They'd better, or Blue Raven would be dancing on their graves. Well, *his* grave anyway, Fargo reflected, since the renegade chief wanted the woman alive.

Rested from the break, their horses galloped with renewed vigor.

Fargo glanced over his shoulder every few yards, counting on the renegades' natural caution to keep them in the tall grass for another five or ten minutes. The half-breed's Sharps boomed again, fainter this time, and he grinned in satisfaction. They still believed he was on the hill.

Susan said nothing until they were safely in the trees and had halted. Then she gazed at him and inquired, "What next?"

"We stay alive."

"Don't you have a plan?"

"We'll ride like hell," Fargo proposed.

"That's it?" Susan responded sarcastically.

"Unless you have any better idea," Fargo said. "Blue Raven will be on our trail in a bit, and since it's daylight he'll be able to track us easily. Now that I know they have a Sharps, I aim to put as much distance between them and us as I can." So saying, he goaded the Ovaro deeper into the forest.

More miles fell behind them, and the morning dragged on. Several hours after leaving the hill they were deep in the heart of the imposing mountains. Fargo decided to follow a game trail that led toward the summit of one. They climbed well above the tree line and halted so he could survey the countryside to their rear.

"I don't see them," Susan commented, her right hand shielding her eyes from the bright sun.

"Me either," Fargo said, puzzled. There were deer and elk scattered here and there, and plenty of hawks and eagles soared on the air currents seeking prey, but the renegades were nowhere in sight.

"Where could they be?"

"I don't know," Skye admitted. "Maybe they had to stop for a while. Their horses were tuckered out."

"So am I," Susan said. "Any chance of us taking a short break?"

"I reckon it won't hurt," Fargo said. The trail they were on wound up and over a rise and as he gazed in that direction, he spied an osprey a few hundred feet beyond. The large hawk abruptly went into a dive, disappearing from view. Fargo rode forward, his curiosity aroused. Unlike other predatory birds, ospreys fed exclusively on fish and consequently were never far from water.

He came to the rise and went a few yards before stopping. Before him spread a small alpine lake, its tranquil surface shimmering like polished glass, rimmed by trees on three sides. The osprey was just climbing into the air, a large fish clutched it its steely talons.

"Oh, my!" Susan exclaimed, and hurried to the water's edge. "Come on," she called back.

Fargo followed her, amused by her antics as she slid down and happily spun in a circle, then stepped to the lake and dipped her right hand in.

"Brrr. It's cold."

"These high country lakes are," Fargo told her. "Half of them stay frozen from October to April."

Susan stood and smiled at him. "Let's go for a swim."

"With Blue Raven after us? Are you crazy?"

"He's miles behind and you know it," Susan stated. "We have the time. And I could really use one. Please."

"If you want to, go—" Fargo began, and stopped in surprise when she set about stripping right in front of his eyes. A moment later her dress fell to the ground, then her underclothes. She stood there in all her sensual splendor, a crimson tinge coloring both cheeks, and beckoned with her right hand.

"Come on. It will be fun."

Thinking that he was as loony as she was, Fargo dismounted and walked toward her, feeling familiar twinges in his loins. "You realize you're playing with fire, don't you?"

Susan Chambers nodded, her eyes twinkling impishly, and stated in a calm voice, "I'm hoping to get burned."

13

Fargo walked up to within inches of her rosy nipples and halted. "Maybe you need more sleep," he joked. "You don't seem to be in your right mind."

"If you only knew," Susan said and suddenly spun, bounded, and dived into the frigid water. She came up sputtering, her golden hair soaked and plastered to her head, a sheen of water glistening on her smiling face. "I'm freezing!" she squealed.

"Then get out," Fargo suggested.

Susan shook her head. "Don't you understand? I need to feel clean again." With that, she pressed her hands together and dived again, moving out to deeper water.

So that was it, Fargo reflected. She hadn't washed since her abduction, and now she was reveling in being able to remove the grime from her soft skin and perhaps something even fouler from the depths of her soul. He grinned, watching her swim and splash and play in innocent abandon. This was the real Susan Chambers, a carefree young woman who enjoyed her life to the fullest.

"Aren't you coming?" she entreated.

"I'd better not," Fargo replied. "One of us has to stay alert in case Blue Raven shows up."

"Chicken," Susan said, pouting, and then she giggled and dived once more.

Fargo saw her slender legs swing into the air and glimpsed the downy triangle of hair at the juncture of her thighs. The temperature seemed to rise by a good ten degrees, and he coughed to clear his throat as he turned and walked to the rise. It wouldn't hurt to check their backtrail one more time, he told himself, glancing over his shoulder.

Susan surfaced, her breasts swaying with the motion of the water, and ran her hands along her hair. She smiled at him and began swimming lazily in a circle.

At the rise he halted and carefully surveyed the land below, observing only abundant wildlife. Off to the southwest was a small herd of buffalo, and the sight brought to mind the many buffalo hunts in which he'd participated when there were many more of the animals than there were now. Those had been the days, riding side by side with his Indian friends, his blood pounding to the rhythm of the mighty beasts' hooves as he rode in close enough to slay a bull Indian-fashion.

He daydreamed, the breeze stirring his hair, and continued to scan the terrain until he heard the light patter of rushing feet. Suddenly a pair of wet, slender arms encircled his waist from behind and a taunting voice whispered up in his ear.

"Are you done stalling?"

"I didn't know I was."

"Am I that ugly, then?" Susan asked, her arms slackening.

Fargo turned, taking in the gorgeous sight of her upturned, pert breasts, her smooth tummy, the seductive curve of her hips, and her exquisite thighs. His breath caught in his throat and when he spoke his voice sounded strained. "You're one of the most beautiful women I've ever laid eyes on."

Susan reached up and cupped her breasts. "Prove it. You claimed that any decent man would be proud to have me as his woman. Well, you're a decent man. So show me."

Fargo saw the intense inner need mirrored in her eyes. Who was he to refuse such a request? He raised his hands, replacing hers on her breasts and slowly massaged them. She flushed crimson, her eyes closing, her lips parting to form a small "o". "I reckon we do have the time," he growled, and planted his lips on her tender mouth.

The kiss was sweet, making Fargo's heart beat wildly. Her nipples became hard under his palms, and she groaned ever so softly. The slick dampness of her skin served to arouse him even further. His tongue probed deep into her mouth and was greeted tentatively by her own. Her scent filled his nostrils and her heavy breathing was sensual music to his ears.

He broke the kiss and let his tongue glide its way down her throat to her left breast. His mouth clamped onto her nipple and he tasted her salty skin. An intense hunger formed within him, eclipsing all other concerns. For the moment nothing mattered except the lovely, yielding woman in his arms.

Fargo tweaked her other breast with his hand, feeling her erect nipple quiver. He kissed and sucked on each globe, letting his hands drift lower until he was insistently stroking her inner thighs.

"Ummmm," Susan moaned.

He inserted the fingers of his right hand between her legs and gently parted her nether lips. She cooed and squirmed and his fingers abruptly became sticky.

"Ohhhhh, Skye."

Fargo used his other hand to undo his gunbelt and lower it to the grass, then he unhitched his pants and they dropped around his ankles. His hard organ brushed against her belly, causing her to open her eyes and look down.

"Oh, my," she breathed.

He put both hands under her arms, lifted her into the air and gradually lowered her down, feeling her legs part and the tip of his manhood brush her pubic hair, then slip into her hot hole. There was no resistance. Susan threw back her head and gasped, her fingers forming into claws which she buried in his arms. Gripping her buttocks, he held her fast and began a pumping motion, rising on his toes again and again as he probed into the heart of her womanhood.

"Uhhhhhh," she grunted. "Oh, God! Oh! I never—knew!"

Fargo took it slow. If she wanted proof that he found her desirable, then he'd damn well give her proof she'd recollect to the end of her days. Lifting her a few inches, he suddenly rammed into her with all of his might.

"Ahhhhhhhh!" Susan cried out and sank her teeth into his shoulder.

The woman had the makings of a first-rate hellcat, Fargo mused, controlling the tempo of his driving thrusts, relishing the friction of her thighs against his. He nibbled on her neck, kissed her full on the mouth, and licked her forehead. She clutched at him as if she never wanted to let go, moving her hips to meet him now, increasing her own pleasure in the bargain.

Fargo squeezed both of her breasts at once, eliciting a

groan from the depths of her throat and a delicious shudder that set his organ tingling. Her hole became an inferno; his organ was on fire. He increased the speed of his thrusts, listening to the slap-slap-slap of their bodies and feeling her breasts grind against his chest.

"Skye!" she called out. "I'm coming! I'm coming!"

He felt her orgasm, felt her spurt inside and the contractions of her belly as she heaved and thrashed in erotic abandon. His organ swelled, and despite his best mental effort to draw out their union even longer, he came with a thunderous quaking of his legs, ramming into her inner softness over and over.

"Aaaaiiieee!" she screeched, panting crazily.

Fargo continued pounding away until his juices were expended and his momentum flagged. He stood still, sheathed in her box, holding her close. Time seemed to stop.

"Thank you," she said softly after a while.

Fargo nodded, then slowly lowered himself down so he could slide out of her. He gave her a last kiss and bent at the waist to pull up his pants. Above him, she inhaled sharply.

"Blue Raven!"

He whirled, straightening as he did, tugging his pants up to his waist. There, approximately three hundred yards from the base of the mountain, were the six renegades. Again an Indian was in the lead doing the tracking. Fargo quickly fastened his pants, buckled on his Colt, and glanced at Susan.

She appeared to be terror stricken, her eyes wide, her hands protectively touching her neck.

"Unless you're partial to traipsing around buck naked, you should get dressed," Fargo prompted.

Susan nodded, then bolted toward the lake.

Fargo sank to his knees, debating his next move. Going back down the mountain would invite certain death, especially since the renegade with the Sharps would pick them off before they reached the bottom. No, his best bet was to let them come to him since he couldn't have asked for a better ambush site if he had planned it that way.

Rising, he ran to the Ovaro. Susan was hurriedly dressing, fumbling with ties and buttons. "Once you're done," he instructed her, "get on your horse and wait." He grabbed the Sharps and removed a box of ammunition from his saddlebags.

"You're fixing to stand and fight?" Susan asked.

"They're riding right into my sights," Fargo said. "I'd be a fool to cut out when I can even the odds a bit more." Turning, he ran back to the rise, being careful to stay below the rim, and knelt. He moved forward until he could see the band again, then placed the cartridges at his side and set about loading the rifle. The renegades were alertly watching the surrounding forest, not paying any special attention to the mountain. So far, the trail had always wound around mountains, not up them.

Their mistake, Fargo reflected, and lay on his stomach. He held the Sharps close to the ground to avoid repeating his own mistake of letting them spot the gleam of sunlight off the gun. Removing his hat, he put it next to the cartridge box. Now he was ready.

The renegades were riding in single file, Blue Raven behind the tracker. As they neared the mountain, the stocky butcher studied it intently, as if his instincts told him something was wrong. When they reached the point where Fargo and Susan had started up, they halted, partially obscured by trees.

Fargo wasn't concerned about being seen. Only his eyes and forehead were above the rim. The renegades were involved in a heated dispute, with much gesturing and loud words. Evidently a few wanted to turn back but Blue Raven had no intention of giving up. Soon they began to climb the slope.

He braced the stock against his shoulder. Once the renegades were clear of the trees, they would be less than one hundred yards away with very little cover available. If he let them get any closer, he might be able to pick them off before they could escape back down the trail. A Sharps was capable of firing four rounds a minute in the hands of someone skilled in its use, and he was one of the best on the frontier.

The band ascended slowly, exercising supreme caution. The Indian in the lead divided his attention between the tracks he was following and the trail ahead. Blue Raven shifted every which way, a cocked rifle in his hands. Behind him came the half-breed armed with the Sharps.

Fargo wanted to take him out of action first, but he didn't have a clear shot. He would have to dispose of the tracker and Blue Raven unless they obligingly fell or dived out of the way. His finger touched the cool trigger, his every nerve on edge.

Out of the trees came the tracker, riding loosely in the saddle, as keenly alert as an Indian could be, which meant he would snap up his gun and fire at the slightest movement.

Lowering his head an inch, Fargo tucked his cheek to the rifle and sighted along the barrel, aiming dead center at the tracker's chest. The hammer clicked as he pulled it back.

Unexpectedly, the Indian in the lead halted and motioned for the other renegades to do likewise. Blue Raven said something; the tracker answered.

Fargo feared that the tracker had somehow spotted him. He could see the Indian eyeing the rim in concern and braced to hear a shout of warning. Instead, the man waved an arm and continued upward. Now they were almost right where Fargo wanted them. He ticked off the yards as they drew nearer, ever nearer, until they were less than fifty yards distant and almost to the spot where he had halted on his way up to scan the countryside.

Then they reached that point and the Indian in the lead abruptly reined up.

There was no resisting a stationary target. Fargo fired. The big rifle boomed, the sound carrying far down the slope as the slug struck the tracker in the chest and lifted him from the saddle to fall lifeless at the feet of Blue Raven's mount.

This time too the renegades didn't panic. Instantly their guns spoke, their weapons aimed at the puff of smoke that marked Fargo's place of concealment.

Skye fed in a fresh cartridge, the acrid gun smoke blowing into his face thanks to the fickle breeze and biting into his lungs when he inhaled. He squinted to see better and went to aim again, expecting the renegades to fan out or retreat. To his consternation, they did neither.

Blue Raven and his cohorts charged.

Fargo had to rush his next shot. The renegades were barreling toward him in an uneven line, Blue Raven slightly to the right of the man with the Sharps. He wanted to neutralize the only weapon they had that was a match for his, so he went for the Sharps carrier next, squeezing off a shot that knocked the stock into his shoulder a hair before the bullet knocked the renegade off his horse.

Only four to go, Fargo told himself, feeding a third round into the rifle while keeping an eye on the onrushing renegades. Their guns were popping like crazy, but the chance of them hitting him when they were being roughly jostled by the motions of their galloping animals was remote. So remote, Fargo discounted it entirely.

He went for his third kill, his finger curling on the trigger. At that moment something slammed into his right temple with the force of a kicking mule, twisting him to the side. Stunned, he knew he'd been hit and tried to straighten, to keep firing. An inky hand seemed to take shape within his mind and enfold it in a constricting grasp, and then he knew nothing at all.

14

The pain revived him.

Fargo grimaced as a wave of acute agony rippled through him. He became vaguely aware of a swaying motion, and that he was lying on his stomach. Then he realized his wrists and ankles were bound. The strong scent of horsehide and the thud of plodding hooves enabled him to guess where he was before he opened his eyes and comfirmed he was draped over a saddle. Over his own saddle, no less, on the Ovaro.

He twisted his head and saw Blue Raven and Susan astride separate horses in front of him. Turning, he found two renegades bringing up the rear. Evidently his third shot had left one less murderous hardcase abroad in the world.

Fargo was immensely surprised to be alive. Not that he objected, but he figured Blue Raven would have gleefully finished him off rather than take him alive. There must be a reason, and the only one he could think of made him almost wish he had been killed.

They were crossing a meadow shrouded by long shadows from adjacent mountains, the sun sinking toward the western horizon to their rear.

He resigned himself to hanging there for a spell. There was nothing he could do anyway, and he could use the time to rest and think. He couldn't tell if the throwing knife was still in his boot. If the renegades had overlooked it, they would pay for the oversight.

A narrow, gurgling stream bordered the meadow on the east. Blue Raven halted, barked orders to his two men in the Sioux language to water the mounts, then swung down and walked up to Susan's horse. Grabbing her waist, he yanked her from the saddle and gave her an angry shove when her feet touched the ground. She tottered but didn't fall, glaring at him in defiance.

Blue Raven drew back his hand to strike her in the face.

"I figured you for a woman beater," Fargo declared to

spare her. "Yellow-bellies like you never tangle with someone your own size in a fair fight."

The renegade chief spun, glowering in rabid hatred, and marched right up to the Trailsman. "So the great Skye Fargo is awake. Good." He spat, hauled off and backhanded Fargo across the mouth.

Pinpoints of anguish exploded in Skye's head and he tasted blood in his mouth. The world spun. He thought he might pass out again. Then he felt rough hands on his shirt and he was dumped onto his side on the ground.

"Don't die on me yet, pig," Blue Raven rasped. "I have plans for you."

Fargo sluggishly rolled onto his back, nausea enveloping him. He lay still until the queasiness subsided, then rose onto his elbows. Blue Raven had returned to Susan and shoved her onto her backside. The two surviving renegades were involved in taking the horses to the stream. None of them seemed particularly concerned about him, perhaps figuring he was no threat with his limbs bound.

Blue Raven walked back and stood smirking down at the big man. "No one has ever given me as much trouble as you, white man. I know why, too. The woman has told me who you are."

"Did she tell you I aim to gut you one day?"

"One of us will be gutted, but it will not be me," Blue Raven declared. He leaned down, grabbed Fargo by the shoulders, and jerked him upright. "Walk or I will kick your ribs in."

Fargo gritted his teeth and shuffled toward Susan. He would have rammed the renegade in the mouth with both fists if he had the strength. A brutal shove sent him stumbling onto his knees, and he swayed as more dizziness assailed him.

"Leave him alone!" Susan snapped.

Blue Raven was on her in a flash, battering her with his open hands. She fell, shielding her face with her forearms, but didn't cry out. "Where did you get this courage all of a sudden?" he demanded. "You were a whimpering dog before."

Susan made no answer, simply glaring up at him, her cheeks red from his blows.

"You want to know something, white bitch?" Blue Raven said. "I'm glad you want to fight back. I like it better when women do." He voiced a brittle, mocking laugh, then moved toward his companions.

Susan scooted over to Fargo and tenderly touched his cheek. "How do you feel?"

"Like I fell off a cliff and landed on my head," Fargo responded.

"I was shocked when I saw you get hit," Susan said. "I tried to help, though. I started to pull out that rifle you stuck in the holster on my horse, but Blue Raven had already reached you. He threatened to shoot you in the head if I didn't give up right then and there."

"You should have lit out."

"And desert you? I couldn't do that."

Fargo tried to give her a stern look, but her friendly smile dissipated his anger. He leaned forward and spoke in a whisper. "I don't know how or when, but I'll try to distract the renegades long enough for you to make your getaway. Be ready."

"I'm not leaving without you," Susan insisted softly.

"Be realistic. You know what they will do to you."

"I don't care. I'm not leaving you and that's final."

He bowed his head, frustrated by her stubbornness but admiring her loyalty. There must be some way to persuade her to go, he reasoned, and hit on an idea. "Listen, we're both dead unless you do as I say. I want you to ride for help when I start a ruckus."

"Where would I find help out here in the middle of the Rockies?"

"Do you remember the spot where you were camped when I freed you?"

"Yes, but I could never find it again in a million years. I'd get lost after going twenty feet."

About to give her directions, to point out the location to prominent landmarks she could use to orient herself, Fargo stiffened when he looked over her shoulder and saw Blue Raven walking toward them.

"I leave you alone for five seconds and you whisper behind my back," the renegade barked, halting next to Susan and cuffing her on the mouth. "What were you talking about?"

Fury seized Fargo and he tried to stand. His body refused to cooperate, his head pounding terribly, and all he could do was rise an inch off his knees before sinking down again.

Blue Raven noticed and snorted in contempt. "Are you in that much of a hurry to die, scout? Don't be. Your time will come soon. I would have cut you into little pieces on that mountain, but all those shots might have drawn any Indians in the area right quick." He paused and placed his hand on a knife on his left hip. "And I don't want anyone to spoil it."

Fargo had figured as much. The butcher would kill him slowly, bit by bit, drawing it out for hours if not days, reveling in his suffering. He couldn't let that happen.

"You can thank your white God that you're getting another day of life," Blue Raven declared, gazing around them. "I want to put more miles behind us tomorrow. When we stop to make camp, that's when the fun will begin."

"You touch him and you'll be sorry," Susan said.

The stocky renegade cackled, then moved off.

"Quit trying to get his goat," Fargo told her. "If you get him riled, I can't do a thing for you while I'm trussed up this way."

"Don't worry. I'll get you loose."

"You'll do no such thing. Don't give them an excuse to kill you, dammit."

Susan recoiled as if slapped again. "You shouldn't talk like that in front of a lady."

Lady? This from the woman who had practically thrown herself at him up by the lake? Fargo closed his eyes, thinking that he should have expected this change in her behavior. Rare was the woman who shared her body with a man and then didn't act as if she owned him afterward. The women in saloons and dance halls were exceptions, but only because once they had their money in hand they were ready to boot the man out the door so the next one could sample their wares and pay up.

The renegades set to work building a fire and securing the horses for the night. They worked for the most part in silence, clearly exhausted from the long pursuit and a lack of food and rest. Twilight had descended when one of the butchers produced jerked venison from a saddlebag and handed out strips to his companions.

"What about us?" Susan asked.

"You go hungry," Blue Raven said. "I want you to beg for your next food."

"Never."

Blue Raven looked at the Trailsman. "Why are white women so dumb? Are they raised that way on purpose so they won't give their men any trouble?"

Susan bristled at the insult. "White women are not dumb, you pig!"

Fearing the renegades would assault her for the slur, Fargo braced to do what little he could to defend her. To his relief, Blue Raven only smirked.

"White women know nothing of life, bitch. You are all pampered like children and think you are more important than you really are. You always have food to eat and nice clothes to wear. You live in warm houses and your men do all the hard work. No wonder white women make such sorry Indian wives."

"You think you know it all," Susan taunted him.

"I know life for what it really is. Hard. Cruel. A life where only the strong survive. Whites are naturally weak, even the men. If it were not for the fact that there are so many of you, the Indian tribes would have driven you back across the Mississippi River many years ago."

"And if it wasn't for men like you giving all Indians a bad name, maybe both sides could learn to live in peace," Susan said.

Blue Raven almost choked on his jerky. "You must be a Bible reader, woman. No one else would say such stupid words. The Indians and the whites will never live in peace. Never."

"Not all men are like you," Susan said. "You're worse than all of them because you go around killing anyone and everyone."

"Whites hate me so I hate them. And Indians who like whites. It is as simple as that," Blue Raven responded.

Fargo wobbled forward on his knees and nudged Susan

with his forehead, hoping to shut her up before she rubbed a nerve and set Blue Raven off. She barely looked at him.

"You know that one day they'll catch up with you," Susan predicted.

"Maybe. But not before I have slit the throats of many more whites, including yours if you do not shut your mouth."

To Fargo's immense relief, Susan took the hint. She glared but said nothing else. Sitting back, he wiggled his right foot and felt the hilt of his throwing knife rub against his lower leg. The renegades weren't as clever as they thought they were. He watched them eating the venison, listening intently as they conversed in Sioux. Since they had no idea he spoke the tongue, they spoke openly.

"Is it safe to drag this white trash along?" asked one of the half-breeds.

"I want to enjoy their deaths," Blue Raven said. "Particularly the Trailsman. He will grovel at my feet by the time I am done."

"And what about those tracks we saw?" inquired the other one.

"What about them?" Blue Raven responded.

"There is a war party in this area. They could come across us at any time. Why slow ourselves down with these whites?"

"Because I say so," Blue Raven stated belligerently, and gave each man a look that dared either of them to challenge his authority. Neither did.

Fargo found the news extremely interesting. The renegades had come across the recent trail of a band of Indians. Small wonder then, that Blue Raven had let him live and departed the lake in haste. There was a good chance the Indians were hostile. He listened to more, to a discussion of the attack on the wagon train and on the Shoshoni village. To his amusement, they were puzzled by his interference in their affairs. They wanted to know the reason and Blue Raven gave them his word that he would extract it through torture.

Darkness gradually shrouded the land. Fargo noticed the renegades kept their fire low as a precaution. Not that the fire in itself posed a danger. Indians were rarely abroad at night and seldom attacked an enemy after the sun set. But they could spot a fire from afar and ride to investigate it the next morning. There were a few exceptions—most notably the fierce Apaches of the Southwest.

Blue Raven announced that a guard should be maintained until morning, and the three renegades decided to take turns keeping watch with Blue Raven pulling the first stint. He sat near the fire the whole time, his rifle cradled in his lap, deep in thought.

Fargo reclined on his side next to Susan, who had curled herself into a ball the moment the two half-breeds laid down to rest. She'd been moodily silent for some time, and he figured it was because she feared being molested again. Thankfully, the renegades made no move to touch her.

He cracked his eyes to watch Blue Raven, hoping the butcher would fall asleep so he could draw the knife from his boot, cut his ropes, and finish off all three. But Blue Raven stayed awake the entire shift, then awakened the next man who took a seat facing Susan and him. As the hours dragged by, Fargo's eyelids became leaden. Despite his best effort, he felt his consciousness drifting away. He shook himself once to no avail, and then a black emptiness claimed his mind for a few minutes. Or so it seemed.

Skye opened his eyes again, certain hardly any time had passed until he realized the third renegade was on guard duty. A faint light to the east heralded the rising of the sun. He had slept for hours. Annoyed at himself, he glanced again at the renegade.

The man was sound asleep!

Instantly Fargo was awake and slowly bending down to reach into his boot. The renegade had his head bowed, his lips fluttering as he snored lightly. Blue Raven and the other killer were deep in slumber. This was the opportunity Fargo had waited for, and he inched his hands under his boot to grip the knife hilt. That was when he felt something touch his shoulder and looked back.

Behind him stood a strapping warrior in beaded buckskins, an arrow nocked to a bow string, the barbed point fixed on his back.

Startled, Fargo lifted his head and slid his fingers out of his boot. He spied other Indians ringing the camp, all with weapons trained on the sleeping figures.

15

There were eight warriors all told. One of them, a lean man carrying a war club, stepped silently forward and stood next to Blue Raven. He placed the end of the club against the renegade's arm, grinned, and prodded it.

Blue Raven came awake with a start, grabbing for the rifle at his side. He glanced up and saw the Indian, a flicker of fear in his eyes. Then he blinked, smiled, and leaped to his feet to give the Indian a hearty hug.

Fargo's hopes sank. For a moment he'd entertained the notion the Indians would turn out to be friendly, but now he knew better. He was trying to identify them by their style of dress and the way in which they wore their long hair, and finally it came to him; they were Bloods. Part of a once supremely powerful confederacy that had controlled virtually all of the northern plains, the Bloods were long-standing allies of the dreaded Blackfeet and the Piegans. Possessing an implacable hatred for all whites, the three tribes had waged ceaseless war against any trappers, troopers, or travelers found in their territory. Fortunately, from the white man's point of view, a series of smallpox epidemics had drastically reduced their numbers and they were no longer considered quite as formidable.

Blue Raven and the man with the war club were chatting like the best of friends. The other two renegades woke up as the rest of the Bloods gathered around.

Of all the luck, Fargo reflected. Had the Indians been Shoshonis, Susan and he could have counted on being released and permitted to go their own way. But now, the danger was merely compounded.

Susan muttered, then abruptly snapped awake and sat up. She saw the Indians, gasped, and glanced at the Trailsman. "Who are they?"

"Bloods. Bad news," Fargo said, not bothering to elaborate on some of the ghastly stories he'd heard about Blood atrocities. They were every bit as savage as Blue Raven and frequently indulged in torture.

"Oh, my," she said softly.

Blue Raven and the Blood leader came over, both snickering as if at some private joke. "You're awake, pretty one," Blue Raven said to Susan. "Good. I would like to introduce a friend of mine."

"Another maggot? Don't waste my time."

"You would do well to keep that sharp tongue of yours quiet," Blue Raven advised her. "He Wolf doesn't speak English, but he can tell a lot from your tone. And if you make him mad, he'll scalp you on the spot."

Susan looked at Fargo, who nodded.

He Wolf reached out, touched her hair, and made a short comment in the Blood tongue.

"He says he has never seen hair like yours," Blue Raven translated.

"Tell him—" Susan began gruffly, reaching up to bat his arm away.

"Don't!" Fargo cautioned, knowing to anger the Blood might result in immediate death.

Susan paused, glaring at the warrior. She lowered her hand reluctantly and muttered, "I don't like being pawed."

Fargo listened to He Wolf and Blue Raven talk. He picked up a few words here and there. Shoshoni was one, and he gathered the renegade was telling about the raid on the village. The Bloods and the Shoshonis were bitter enemies and He Wolf would be pleased at the news.

The renegades broke out their jerked venison, sharing pieces with the Bloods. A five minute talk ensued, and at the end Blue Raven turned to his prisoners and announced: "I hope you are feeling sociable."

"Why?" Susan replied.

"Because I've agreed to go to He Wolf's village, which makes you a lucky woman."

"How do you figure?"

Blue Raven smirked. "I can sell you to the Bloods for horses and guns. By this time tomorrow you could be the bride of a Blood warrior."

"Never!"

"There you go, being dumb again," Blue Raven snapped. "Would you rather be killed?"

Susan made no answer.

Putting his palms on the grass, Fargo pushed to his knees. He glanced at the warrior who had crept up behind him, wondering if the man suspected the reason he had stuck his fingers into his boot. The warrior was talking to a renegade, who then turned and whispered into Blue Raven's ear.

Without uttering a word Blue Raven stepped up to Fargo and shoved him onto his side. Leaning down, the stocky butcher reached into Skye's right boot and drew out the sheath. "What have we here?" he said to no one in particular, wagging the weapon in the air.

Fargo knew resistance would be futile. He was watching Blue Raven's angry features; he barely glimpsed the sweeping foot that slammed into his ribs, spearing torment into his chest. Doubling over, he inhaled raggedly.

"Try to trick me, you bastard," Blue Raven growled. "You'll get yours soon enough." He rejoined He Wolf.

Lying still, Fargo waited for the pain to subside. He felt Susan's hands touch his cheek and glanced up. "I'm fine," he said in response to the concern mirrored in her eyes. For a while, anyway, he told himself. Because he could guess what would happen next, and it would make escape almost impossible.

Blue Raven looked at them and announced, "We are going to He Wolf's village. If either of you try anything, you will not live to reach it."

Fargo heard Blue Raven direct a renegade to cut his bonds so he could ride. The man came over, pulled a knife, and sliced the rope with two strokes. Refusing to lie there and let them gloat over his discomfort, Fargo sat up.

He Wolf turned to the nearby trees and whooped three times. Seconds later two more Bloods appeared, both mounted and leading the horses belonging to their companions.

"What can we do?" Susan whispered. "If they get us to their village, it'll be hopeless."

"We'll find a way out of this fix," Fargo assured her, more to soothe her anxiety than from any firm conviction that they could turn the tables on their captors.

In due course everyone was on horseback. Blue Raven and

He Wolf took the lead, followed by Fargo and Susan, then the renegades and the Blood warriors. They headed to the north at a brisk pace.

Fargo stayed alert for any occasion to make a break for it. Unfortunately, He Wolf stuck to generally open ground, avoiding dense forest where a bid might be possible. He noticed that Blue Raven had the Sharps and other objects, probably including the .44, rolled up in a blanket behind the renegade's saddle. The familiar stock protruded from one side, and he was strongly inclined to make an insane grab for it.

Their course led them into a low mountain range, winding along until they came to a broad plain. To the east, erected near a river, were sixty-three lodges, all buffalo hide tepees, many decorated with gaily painted symbols. Warriors, women, and playful children were everywhere, engaged in various activities. A shout went up when the approaching party was spotted and Bloods converged on the edge of the village.

Fargo saw hostility on many faces. A circle of Bloods formed around Susan and him as the Indians conversed in subdued voices. He knew any one of the warriors would glee-fully slit his throat and take his scalp. His time left to live could be measured in hours.

An elderly Blood stepped forward to cordially greet Blue Raven. Instructions were barked, and several warriors walked up to the Ovaro and motioned for the big man to climb down.

"What about me?" Susan asked.

"Don't move unless you're told to," Fargo said as he dismounted. "And whatever you do, don't get any of these Indians angry." He was promptly gripped by the upper arms and hustled toward a tepee thirty feet away.

"Skye!" Susan called out.

"Don't panic," Fargo cautioned, not having anything better to tell her. When they reached the tepee one of the warriors opened the flap. Fargo ducked his head to enter. Snickering, two of them gave him a rough push, causing him to stumble to his knees, and the flap closed, leaving him alone in the dim interior. Except for sunshine filtering through the ventilation opening at the top of the lodge, there was no light.

He waited for his eyes to adjust and discovered items arranged along the base of the lodge walls: blankets, a buffalo robe, tin pans, parfleches, and more. Suddenly a terrified scream erupted outside and he scrambled to the flap and shoved it open.

Several Bloods were taking Susan Chambers toward another lodge to the south. She was resisting as best she could, trying to tear her wrists from their grasp while kicking at their shins. They barely paid attention, shoving her into the dwelling and then taking up guard posts outside, their features inscrutable.

At least he knew where to find her when the time came to make his break, Fargo mused. The thought prompted a lopsided grin. He was becoming terribly optimistic in his young age. Turning, he walked to the parfleches and examined their contents. Constructed from rawhide and adorned with elaborate, colorful beadwork, parfleches served as the Indian equivalent of drawers and closets. There were three in the tent. The first contained herbs and wild onions; the second was a woman's sewing bag and held her awls, beads, quills, grasses, sinew thread, and bone needles. The third contained a few strips of dried venison.

He'd eat after all. Fargo settled down and greedily consumed every last morsel. He rooted in the bottom of the bag but found no more. Then he stepped over to the remains of a cooking fire in the center of the floor. The coals were cold. The owners of the lodge must be away somewhere, which accounted for its selection as his temporary prison.

Having examined everything there was to examine, Fargo moved to the entrance and cautiously parted the flap again. There were two warriors a few feet away, their backs to the tepee, conversing. He could see Blue Raven and the elderly Blood, who he guessed must be the chief, walking toward a lodge two dozen yards to the north. His eyes narrowed when the Ovaro and Susan's stallion were both ground-hitched outside that lodge and the two leaders went inside.

Interesting, Fargo thought. If he could get Susan out, and if they could reach the horses, they stood a slim prayer. But how to do it? That was the big question.

He sat there for hours. No one paid him a visit. From the lodge containing Blue Raven and the elderly Blood came raucous laughter. Warriors entered and left constantly. Women took in food.

The morning gave way to afternoon. Fargo became drowsy and paced to ward off fatigue. Every so often he would gaze out. Once he spied two women taking food into Susan's lodge. Angry curses greeted their arrival. Moments later they fled the tepee, the food following them out in flight. He chuckled and resumed pacing.

By the time the sun was close to the western horizon, the celebration in the chief's lodge was loud enough to be heard throughout the entire village. Fargo knelt near the flap, feeling like a caged animal, his nerves rubbed raw.

Unexpectedly, out came Blue Raven, the elderly Blood, He Wolf, and two other warriors. They headed toward him.

Fargo lowered the flap and scooted to the rear, casting about desperately for something he could use as a weapon. The tin pans were the only metal objects at hand, and he figured he'd be damned if he was going to go out of the world flailing away with a lousy cooking implement.

Suddenly the flap opened. In walked Blue Raven, He Wolf, and the chief.

"Hello, Fargo, you son of a bitch," Blue Raven said, smiling and swaying slightly from the effects of the alcohol he'd been drinking most of the day.

"Took you long enough," Fargo said, tensing his legs to make a leap for the entrance once they closed in.

"Did what?" Blue Raven said, then laughed. "No, fool. We're not here for that. It's not quite time."

"Then why are you here?"

"To gloat," Blue Raven declared sadistically. "You see, I've struck a good bargain with my old friend here, Chief Iron Tail." He indicated the elderly Blood. "Would you like to hear?"

"No."

"I'll tell you anyway," Blue Raven said, exposing all his teeth in a wicked sneer. "I've traded him for ten of their best horses, four rifles, ammunition, and enough whiskey to keep me supplied for a month."

"Lucky you," Fargo said bitterly, wondering what the man was leading up to.

"And guess what I traded?" Blue Raven asked, then answered his own question. "He gets the blond bitch, to do with as he pleases. He also gets your pinto." He paused, the sneer widening. "And you."

"Me?"

Blue Raven nodded. "The Bloods are holding a special celebration tonight and you'll be the guest of honor. Of course, you'll be tied to stakes during the festivities, but you won't mind so much by the time they are done skinning you alive."

So that was it. Torture and worse. Fargo felt rage building within him and bunched his big hands into fists.

"Just thought you would like to know," Blue Raven said and cackled. He turned to the flap, unable to resist a parting taunt over his right shoulder. "Enjoy the time you have left, white man. In one hour they are coming for you."

16

One hour! Fargo watched the flap close behind them and resumed his pacing. He had to come up with a plan, some way of getting the hell out of there before the hour was up. Rushing the guards was out of the question. Other Bloods were bound to see him and give the alarm. Secrecy and stealth were in order if he was to have any hope of also saving Susan.

But how?

Think! he goaded himself. There had to be a way. Again he scanned the interior, noting the various items. Since he couldn't make a break for it, maybe he could trick the Bloods when they came to get him. He stared at the buffalo robe and the blankets, an idea taking shape.

It would all depend on how many came for him, Fargo realized. If only two or three, the idea just might work. He quickly brought the blankets and the robe to the center of the lodge, behind where the cooking fire had been, and squatted. First he rolled the blankets up and tried to stand them on end. Both toppled over. Returning to the side, he carried over an armful of parfleches, then did the same with the tin pans, being careful not to have them clang and attract the attention of the warriors outside.

He stacked the parfleches in a pile and propped the pans against the rear of the rawhide bags for added support. Next he took the rolled blankets and leaned both against the front of the bags, aligning them so they would stay upright. Finally he took the heavy buffalo robe, draped it over the whole affair, and tucked the robe tight to give the illusion he wanted.

Moving to the entrance, Fargo gave his handiwork a critical inspection. In the dark, and from a distance of eight feet or so, the shadowy arrangement might be mistaken for a kneeling man. Not for long, of course, but it could buy him the few precious seconds he'd need to jump whoever entered.

Now all he had to do was wait. He squatted beside the flap and peeked out. Both warriors were still there, as were the pair of guards outside Susan's lodge. He gazed at the chief's tepee, knowing the order to fetch him would come from there. The minutes went by with agonizing slowness, and he found himself rubbing his palms together or tapping his fingers against his legs to release his nervous energy.

After an eternity someone emerged from Iron Tail's tepee and came toward his. He recognized the man as He Wolf and there could be no doubt why the warrior was coming. Rising, he stepped to the right of the flap and placed his back to the buffalo hide wall. It was the only blind spot in the entire lodge. When He Wolf and the guards entered, they would first see his makeshift figure in the middle and hopefully never glance around and spot him.

Shortly, Fargo heard voices and then the flap began to swing inward as someone entered. He believed it was one of the guards. The warrior looked straight ahead, seeing the decoy, and came all the way in, straightening and taking two strides. Behind this first Blood came He Wolf, who moved to the right to pass the guard. Finally, the other guard stepped inside, still slightly bent at the waist.

He Wolf stopped and addressed the makeshift figure in a haughty tone.

Which served as Fargo's cue to swing into action. He took a step, his right fist whipping up and in, striking the second guard on the tip of the chin with all of his might. Teeth crunched, blood sprayed, and the man toppled soundlessly.

Both He Wolf and the first guard started to turn.

Fargo punched the first guard on the ear, his knuckles slamming into the man's head and knocking the warrior off his feet. In a swift step he reached He Wolf just as the Blood faced him. He Wolf's mouth opened; he was about to shout for aid. Fargo couldn't let that happen. With a brutal flick of his right leg, he planted his foot in He Wolf's groin.

The lean warrior doubled over, clutching protectively at his privates and sputtering wildly.

Not letting up for an instant, Fargo drove a right-left combination into He Wolf's face, reducing the man's lips and nose to pulp, flattening He Wolf to the ground. Whirling, he discovered the first guard was rising. He took a step and kicked the man full in the mouth, catapulting the Blood into the decoy.

Fargo shifted right and left, ready to continue the fight, but he was the only one still moving. All three Bloods were unconcious. He Wolf gurlged and twitched.

He quickly went to the flap and checked outside. There was no commotion, no outcry. No one had heard. The guards near Susan's lodge were chatting and laughing. He'd done it. Elated, he went to the Bloods, hunting for weapons. On each man he found a knife, nothing else. Disappointed, he wedged all three blades under the front of his leather belt, then hastened to the decoy and donned the bulky buffalo robe. If he held his head low he might pass for a Blood, provided he stayed away from the village campfires.

Fargo thought of his hat, lost somewhere back on the mountain where he'd been shot, and resolved to buy a new one as soon as he hit civilization. Holding the robe tight to his body, he went to the flap once more. He peered out, and moments later when both guards at Susan's lodge looked in the opposite direction, he slipped out and walked rapidly to the north, circling around the tepee where he had been held and coming at them from due east.

Neither Blood gave him a second glance. They were smiling contentedly, perhaps looking forward to the up-coming festivities. Fargo clamped his chin to his chest and deliberately walked a bit unsteadily, as if he had started celebrating early. The ruse worked. Both guards stared at him and snickered.

Fargo placed each hand on a knife hilt. He angled toward Susan's lodge, pretending to nearly fall.

The guards thought his antics were hilarious.

He slowed to glance both ways. To the northwest were several women, their arms laden with broken branches, hurrying deeper into the village. Pausing, he let them get almost out of sight, then advanced. There was no one else around.

Fargo made straight for the lodge. One of the guards said something in the Blood language, probably telling him to stay away, but he kept going. Out of the corner of his eye he saw the guards move to intercept him. Neither appeared alarmed; they assumed he was a harmless drunk. He let them reach the entrance first. Let them pivot toward him and then, when he was a mere yard off, he lunged, a knife sweeping out in each hand.

The Bloods were caught unawares.

He speared a keen blade into each man, buryng each knife to the hilt in a yielding stomach, slanting the blades upward as he struck and savagely twisting them. Both Bloods involuntarily grunted and grabbed at his steely arms, but it was too late.

The Blood on the left sagged, expelling a long breath as he did. On the right, the other warior seemed to go into shock, his eyes the size of walnuts as he feebly yanked at the Trailman's forearm.

Fargo never stopped. To any casual observer it must appear as if a drunken warrior collided with the guards and all three tumbled to the grass. He shoved, surprised at how easily both men went down, and landed on his knees between them within inches of the flap.

A swift look to his rear showed there were few Bloods abroad in his immediate vicinity, and none were headed in his direction. He figured practically everyone was in a lodge either eating or preparing for the night's event.

Fargo held each guard down until both stopped moving. Leaving the knives buried in their bodies, he scooted to the flap and pushed it open. The interior was as inky as his own had been. To his dismay, a shout loud enough to rouse the dead arose within.

"Get out of here, you rotten heathen, or I'll scratch your eyes out!"

"Susan, it's me," Fargo whispered, hoping no one came to investigate. "Pipe down, you idiot."

"Skye!"

He saw her rush toward him and barely had time to brace his legs before she plowed into him, throwing her slim arms around his neck.

"Thank God! I thought you were one of the Bloods!" Susan exclaimed.

"If you don't keep quiet, we'll have *all* of the Bloods after us," Fargo cautioned gruffly, giving her a fleeting embrace.

"Sorry," Susan said in his ear. "I'm just so damn glad to see you."

"I understand, but we must move fast," Fargo told her. He twisted, grabbed one of the dead guards by the shoulders, and hurriedly pulled the man into the tepee. The buffalo robe nearly slipped off his shoulders.

"Is there anything I can do?" Susan asked.

"Get set to make a break for it," Fargo replied, and seized the second warrior. He surveyed the village and spied a camp dog a dozen yards off, eyeing him curiously. Afraid it might begin barking crazily and alert the entire tribe, he dragged the body out of sight and crouched near the flap.

"Blue Raven stopped by," Susan mentioned in a whisper. "He bragged that he had traded me to the Blood chief." She paused. "He claimed I would be lucky too live out the year."

"We'll both live a lot longer if we can reach our horses," Fargo said. Peeking out, he saw the dog leaving. The Ovaro, Susan's stallion, several horses that undoubtedly belonged to Iron Tail, and Blue Raven's own animal were still near the chief's tepee.

"How can we get there without being seen?" she inquired nervously.

"I'm going to step out and turn. When I open the robe, slide out and stand under it with me."

"Won't we be a little obvious?"

"No. Indians do it all the time. It's customary for a brave and a maiden who are courting to stand under a robe together. They make small talk and walk around a bit, but they usually stay close to her father's lodge."

"That's the Indian idea of courting?"

"In some tribes," Fargo said. "Now let's get going." He cautiously exited the lodge and instantly spun, opening the robe wide. She was out and pressed flush with his body in the blink of an eye. Folding the robe around her, he turned and headed for their horses.

"I'm scared to death," Susan confided, her voice barely audible.

"Just make sure that whatever happens, you don't cry out," Fargo instructed her.

"I won't," she promised.

They covered half the distance to the chief's lodge when the flap opened, filling the night with boisterous voices and laughter, and a lone Blood emerged. The man hitched at his pants and went to depart, then halted, his gaze on the buffalo robe.

Fargo decided to brazen it out. He abruptly halted, took Susan into his arms, and planted a lingering kiss on her warm lips. Thankfully, she responded ardently. He glanced at the warrior while his tongue touched hers, seeing the Blood smirk and move off. Letting go, he hustled her forward.

"What was that for?" Susan whispered.

"Old time's sake," Fargo said, intently watching the flap. If other Bloods emerged when they were in the act of mounting, they might not make it out of the village. He went faster, looping his right arm around her slender waist and practically carrying her the rest of the way, making for her stallion first. As soon as they reached it, he placed his hands under her arms and swung her into the saddle. "Stay low," he warned, stepping to the Ovaro.

Suddenly he remembered the bundle on Blue Raven's mount. He went to the horse, reached up, and found the rolled-up blanket still tied behind the saddle. Using the last of the knives he had taken from the Bloods, he sliced the ties and lowered the bundle to the grass. Inside was his Sharps, the .44, his throwing knife in its sheath and, slightly the worse for wear because it had been crumpled up, his hat. His fingers flew as he reclaimed each article. With the Colt in its holster, the Arkansas toothpick snug inside his boot, and the hat on his head, he grasped the Sharps in his left hand and shrugged out of the heavy robe.

More loud laughter issued from within the chief's lodge.

Fargo paused, half-expecting Bloods to pour out. But the laughter subsided, followed by the subdued sounds of conversation. He returned to the Ovaro and placed the rifle in the saddle holster. Relief flooded through him as he stuck his right boot in the stirrup, grabbed the pommel, and forked the saddle.

Susan straightened, her features pale in the moonlight. Motioning with his left arm, Fargo goaded the Ovaro into a walk, aware that a galloping horse would attract unwanted attention. He went only a few yards, then stopped as someone materialized directly in his path.

A woman appeared, hastening toward Iron Tail's tepee. She spied the horses, looked up at the rider, and halted in astonishment.

Fargo knew she would scream her lungs out in another moment. Since gunfire would alert the Bloods as surely as her scream, he didn't bother shooting her. Instead, he spurred the pinto ahead, swerving to go past her.

Not so Susan Chambers. She lashed her stallion into a run, her mount slamming into the shocked Blood just as the woman threw back her head and screeched, sending the woman flying through the air to crash onto her back.

Then they were in the clear, Fargo in the lead. He looked back to see Indians spilling from almost every lodge. Once again his luck had run true to form—namely bad. Because now every warrior in the village would be hot on their trail.

17

To a chorus of angry yells and confused shouts, Fargo galloped out of the village and bore due south toward the low mountain range, Susan riding on his right. He rode recklessly, aware that every moment was vital, planning to put as much distance between them and the Bloods as he could.

Already pursuit was being organized. Someone was shouting instructions and warriors were racing to their horses.

Fargo repeatedly glanced back, judging the progress of their escape bid. The stark outline of the range was still a quarter of a mile off when a huge body of warriors poured out of the village and sped in the same direction.

"They're coming!" Susan exclaimed.

"Ride for your life," Fargo advised, doing precisely that. If he fell into the hands of the Bloods now, after killing those guards, he could expect the most horrible fate imaginable.

The Ovaro had enjoyed a lengthy rest and flowed effortlessly over the rugged ground. Susan's stallion was hard-pressed to keep up.

Fargo raced onward until they entered the range and followed a narrow valley to the southeast. Rearing above them on both sides were steep, inky slopes. Occasionally they heard loud crashing noises as animals fled through the thick undergrowth at their approach.

All the while, to their rear, the murderous Bloods whooped excitedly.

"Can we lose them?" Susan asked.

"We'll try," Fargo replied, avoiding a boulder in his path at the very last second, swinging to the right to force her horse to also go around.

They came to a fork in the valley. Fargo reined up, debating which branch to take. From the noise of their pursuers, he estimated they had a seven or eight hundred yard lead. Since the Bloods were relying on sight, following the lingering puffs of dust raised by the Ovaro and Susan's mount, he could shake them by a simple ploy. Temporarily, anyway. Because once the Bloods realized they had lost the trail, the warriors would separate into small groups and fan out, scouring the countryside.

He bore to the left, moving slower so as not to raise dust clouds, and traveled only fifty feet before cutting to the right into a stand of saplings. Threading the pinto among the thin trees, he penetrated well into the stand and halted.

Susan stopped close beside him and whispered, "What if this doesn't work?"

"Then by midnight I'll be trying to stuff my innards back into my belly and Iron Tail will be slobbering all over you."

She frowned, then reached out to touch his arm. "I'm scared," she admitted.

"You're doing fine," Fargo told her.

"Only because you're here. Without you, I'd be too scared to do a thing."

The shrieking Bloods reached the fork and drew up.

Peering through the saplings, Fargo could just distinguish the warriors and their milling horses and hear the heated debate that ensued as they tried to determine which way to go. Finally they divided in half, each group taking a branch, and broke into a gallop. He tensed, his right hand on the Colt, watching them sweep past his hiding place. If the Ovaro or Susan's horse should whinny loudly, their lives would be forfeit.

Over two dozen Bloods pounded away into the night.

Fargo waited a suitable interval, then moved to the edge of the trees. The cool breeze fanned the sweat on his brow. He let the Bloods get farther and farther off, until the noise they made was almost too faint to be heard, and rode into the open.

"We did it!" Susan declared happily.

"We did nothing," Fargo corrected her. "We won't be safe until we're twenty miles or more from the village." He turned to the right, going in the same direction as the Indians.

"I won't *feel* safe until I'm back at the wagon train," Susan commented. "Even then, I'd rather be back in Ohio than anywhere else."

"Why is your pa headed for Oregon?" Fargo asked softly, thinking the conversation would soothe her jangled nerves.

"He wants to make a new life for us," Susan said. "He was a clerk at a store and they let him go without any warning. It made him furious. He says he's tired of working for folks who don't appreciate a good man when they have one on the payroll. So we're going to Oregon where we'll take up farming and be our own bosses."

"Farming is hard work. It's not for everybody."

"Pa was born and raised on a farm. Said he's a fool for ever having left it."

"And what about you?" Fargo asked.

"Me?" Susan said, and smiled wistfully. "I reckon I'll try to find a decent man who will treat me right and provide a good home for our family." She glanced at him. "Someone who won't mind putting down roots."

"You have me pegged," Fargo admitted.

"I'm not a worldly woman by any stretch," Susan said, "but I know enough about men to know one who has the wanderlust when I meet him. It'll be years, if ever, before a woman throws a loop wide enough to rope you in."

Fargo chuckled. "You reckon so?"

"I know so. In spite of that, you're the kind of man most women would like to get acquainted with. You're like the candy in a store display. You're tempting, good-looking, and sweet as can be when you put your mind to it. You're irresistible to women who have a craving for handsome men, even though they know you'll ride out of their lives before too long."

He said nothing. For a filly, she certainly did know a lot about the relationships between men and women.

"I'll always treasure my memories of you," Susan concluded.

"Just so we stay alive long enough to have memories," Fargo said.

They continued in silence for over an hour. The sounds of the Bloods had long since faded when they came to a ridge and began to climb it. In the distance a coyote howled. A bit later a second coyote answered.

"Were they wolves?" Susan asked nervously.

"Coyotes."

"How can you tell the difference?"

"Wolves have a lower, steadier, shorter howl."

"You know a lot about the wildlife out here, don't you?"

"I've lived on the frontier all of my adult life. After a while identifying the animals becomes second nature."

Susan surveyed the benighted landscape. "I could never live out here in the middle of nowhere. It's too spooky for my tastes."

Grinning, Fargo glanced at the rim a few dozen feet above. He skirted a pine tree and arched his back to relieve a slight cramp. What he wouldn't give for a full night's sleep, he reflected.

Susan fell a few yards behind.

Not until Skye was almost to the top did he hear the heavy thud of slowly plodding hooves. He abruptly reined up, but he was too late. Coming toward him up the opposite side was an Indian on foot, a Blood, leading a horse that limped.

The warrior spied the big man at the same moment. He instantly halted and began to slip a bow from his left shoulder.

Fargo couldn't cut to the right or the left for fear of the Blood shooting Susan. Fleeing invited a shaft in the back. There was only one recourse, and he employed it. His right hand flashed the .44 out as the Blood grabbed an arrow, and he thumbed the hammer back.

The warrior started to nock the shaft to his bow string.

His hands a blur, Fargo fanned the revolver twice. The slungs caused the warrior to totter backward down the slope and crash against a tree. The Blood sank to the ground and was still.

"What happened?" Susan cried.

Fargo moved forward until he could see that the warrior was indeed dead, then holstelred the Colt and returned to her side. "One of the Bloods was on his way back to the village. I figure his horse came up lame."

"The others will have heard the shots," Susan said.

"I know," Fargo said and added a forceful. "Damn!"

"So what now?"

"This way," Fargo said, riding to the right. The ridge

would be swarming with Bloods before too long and he had to find another safe spot to hide before then.

Riding along the crest until they came to the east slope, they made their way to the bottom at a canter. For the next hour and a half they rode on without mishap. They came to a spacious plain and promptly started across.

Fargo cocked his head but heard nothing to indicate the Bloods were on their trail. Instead, from their left, close at hand, arose a feral growl. He twisted and spied several shifting shapes loping along close to the ground thirty feet away, pacing the horses.

Susan looked and asked in an unconcerned tone, "More coyotes?"

"No. Wolves."

"Really?" Susan said, concern in her voice now. "I didn't think wolves would come this close to people."

"Usually they don't."

"What do they want?"

"I don't know," Fargo said, puzzled by the strange behavior. The wolves must be curious, he reasoned. Wolves rarely attacked humans. If starving or rabid they might, but otherwise they knew enough to stay away from white men with their loud guns or Indians with their deadly bows. So what were six or seven wolves doing out there?

He recollected hearing about three trappers who had made a camp up by the Tetons one summer. A pack of wolves had surrounded the fire and sat there staring at the men. None of the trappers had been too concerned until, without warning, the pack closed in. A furious fight had claimed the lives of one of the trappers and five wolves. The rest had then melted away. No one ever knew what provoked the attack.

Fargo didn't like being shadowed. He brought the Ovaro to a gallop, being careful not to draw away from Susan who was riding with her back as stiff as a board. A few shots might drive the pack off he figured, but the shots would let the Bloods know where to find them. So he simply kept going.

The wolves paced the horses all the way to the end of the

plain. Then they unexpectedly ran to the northwest and soon disappeared.

"Thank goodness," Susan breathed.

Before them was a narrow strip of woodland at the base of a high cliff. Fargo rode into the woods until he came to the sheer rock precipice and reined up. They needed somewhere to lay low for a short spell, and having the cliff at their backs meant he only had to keep watch in one direction. He turned to the right, proceeding along the boulder-strewn base until he reached an overhang. "This will do," he announced, swinging down.

"We're stopping?" Susan asked gratefully, and dismounted before he could answer. She walked a few feet, her legs stiff, her back slightly stooped. "My poor body can use a break. I'm not used to being in the saddle so much."

Fargo stepped over and cupped her chin. "You ride better than many men I know."

"Why, thank you, kind sir," Susan said with an impish grin. She suddenly pressed her body against his and molded his mouth with her lips.

Savoring her warmth and the feel of her jutting breasts, Fargo embraced her and let his hands play over her back. In the back of his mind he weighed the risk of taking the time to give free rein to his surging passion. Already he was hard and growing, and he ground into her mound with a thrust of his hips.

Susan broke the kiss. "Mmmmm. Nice. Too bad we can't go all the way."

"Who says we can't?" Fargo responded, and brought his hands around to fondle her bosom.

"Skye," she said. "Not here."

"Why not?" Fargo asked, lowering his lips to her tender throat.

"The Bloods," Susan said, beginning to breathe heavily.

"They're at least an hour behind us, likely more," Fargo answered, and nibbled on her right ear.

"That tickles," Susan said, squirming delightfully. She placed her hands on his broad shoulders. "What about the wolves?"

"They were just curious and they're a mile away by now," Fargo said, his organ now threatening to burst his pants. There was something about the idea of taking her then and there, while they were on the run, alone in the dark that stirred him to a fever pitch. Maybe it was the excitement, the element of danger. Whatever, he squeezed her nipples through the fabric of her dress until she panted and groaned.

"I want you," Fargo said harshly, and reached down to hike her dress up to her hips. He stroked her velvet thighs, feeling her legs quiver in arousal, and sank his tongue deep into her mouth.

Susan clamped her body to his.

Fargo could barely restrain himself. A fire consumed him, and he swooped his right hand between her legs to discover the feeling was mutual. Her silken box was an inferno ready to receive him. He gladly obliged her, undoing his pants and pressing his manhood to her soft legs.

"Oh, Skye," Susan gasped. "Ohhhhhhh."

He'd had enough of the preliminaries. In a smooth motion he rammed his organ into her womanhood all the way to the hilt, and felt her squirm as she threw her head back and moaned.

"Yessss! I want you one more time!"

Not about to disappoint her, Fargo pounded away, rising on the balls of his feet to bury himself in the depths of her slit. He pumped and pumped, his mouth on hers, his hands holding her around the waist for support, hearing her breath whoosh from her nostrils, their bodies moving faster and faster until they both exploded at the same time.

"Ahhhhhhhhh! Wonderful!" she blurted.

Fargo couldn't agree more.

18

The harsh chattering of a squirrel brought Fargo's head up with a snap and he blinked in the dim morning sunlight. He rose from where he sat underneath the overhang and stretched, the Sharps held in his right hand. To his left, sleeping peacefully, was Susan.

He walked a few yards into the trees, peering at the expanse of open ground they had crossed the night before. There was still no sign of the Bloods, which perplexed him no end. He'd figured the Indians would be after them as soon as the body of the slain Indian was discovered. But despite staying awake until the wee hours before dawn, the Bloods had failed to appear. And all he'd heard were the wolves howling in the distance.

Could it be Iron Tail and the rest had figured trying to catch them at night was a hopeless cause, so the Bloods had made camp, planning to resume the hunt at first light? It was the only reason that made any sense to Fargo. He returned to Susan and squatted, admiring the way her breasts rose and fell as she slept. Reluctantly, he gave her shoulder a shake.

She opened her eyes, stared into his, and smiled dreamily. "I slept like a baby thanks to you," she said.

"What did I do?"

"Made me so relaxed and sleepy, I had no trouble falling asleep for the first time in days."

"Glad to be of service," Fargo said. "But now we've got to light out again. Are you up to it?"

"Are you kidding?" Susan rejoined, sitting up. "I won't feel completely safe until we reach the wagon train."

Fargo helped her up. Minutes later both stallions were saddled and he was swinging onto the Ovaro. She came out of the undergrowth after attending to her "business," as she called it, and climbed on her mount. "I know this will be rough on you," he told her, "but the harder we push today, the sooner we're out of Blood country."

Susan grinned. "Don't sit there jabbering. I'll be right behind you."

Turning the Ovaro southward, Fargo rode along the base of the cliff, paralleling the plain for half a mile. The woods broadened, becoming a green sea of pine trees, the carpet of brown needles underfoot dampening the noise made by their animals. He deliberately stayed in the denser vegetation, reckoning that the Bloods would expect them to stick to the open ground where they could make better time.

Six miles from the overhang he spied the first band of Bloods and instantly reined up. There were only five of the warriors going in the opposite direction, crossing over a high hill to the west.

Susan saw and whispered, "Why are there only five?"

"They've broken up into small groups so they can cover more territory quicker."

"If they don't find us by tonight, will they give up?"

"We can always hope," Fargo responded, riding on, extra cautious since where there was one group there might well be another nearby. He reached a small meadow and went around it, keeping well back in the trees.

"Skye?"

"What is it?"

"Will you do me a favor?" Susan asked.

Fargo looked back at her. "What kind of favor?"

"If the Bloods do spot us and we end up trapped, with no way out, would you—" Susan said haltingly and broke off, unable to complete the statement.

"Get those thoughts out of your head. We'll make it."

"I don't want any of them to put their hands on me," Susan said. "I couldn't take that."

Her strained tone touched Fargo. After all she had been through, he could understand how she felt. But he balked at the notion of shooting her. The idea of just giving up on life went against his grain. As long as there was breath in his body he would fight back against anyone out to harm him.

Suddenly, off to the right a horse whinnied.

Fargo halted and gestured for Susan to do the same. He scanned the forest, spotting no one. The seconds crawled by and he stayed put, stroking the Ovaro's neck to keep it quiet. Then he detected movement far into the trees, and leaning forward he glimpsed a half-dozen warriors riding northward in single file.

Susan's stallion unexpectedly snorted.

His right hand dropping to his Colt, Fargo tensed, waiting to see if any of the Bloods had heard. The warriors kept going, though, and were soon out of sight. He straightened and glared at her horse. "If he does that again, I'll slit his throat and you can ride double with me."

"You wouldn't."

"Try me," Fargo said, moving out once more.

They rode hard for hours. Noon found them at a stream and Fargo called a halt. He watered both animals while Susan sat down with her back to a tree and fussed with her hair. From where he stood he could see grassland ahead and beyond, a range of stark, rocky mountains.

Something moved on the grassland.

Instantly, Fargo pulled both horses away from the water and into cover. He tied them to branches, tugged out the Sharps, and stepped back to the stream, crouching so he would blend into the background.

"What's the matter?" Susan asked.

"Don't know yet," Fargo said. "Stay with the horses until I get back." He started to move forward.

"You're not leaving me here alone?"

"I won't be long," Fargo assured her, breaking into a run. His boots smacked on the hard ground as he covered the fifty yards to the end of the forest. Darting behind a trunk, he rose and searched for the cause of the movement. He didn't have to search very hard.

There were six riders to the southwest, riding along the stream toward him. Five were Bloods, and one of them was Chief Iron Tail. The last rider wore an old army coat, a dark beaver hat, and a red scarf.

Blue Raven.

Fargo cocked the Sharps. Twice now he'd tried to kill that son of a bitch, and twice he'd been thwarted. But not again. If he let Blue Raven live now—if he simply rode off—then every innocent life that the renegade took in the future would be on Fargo's head. This was his last chance to end it once and for all.

He thought of Susan, regretting he didn't have time to explain. If things went wrong, she wouldn't last long by herself. If things went right, they'd be miles away before more Bloods arrived. He hoped.

There was another reason to make a stand, Fargo reflected. If he could also slay the chief, the Bloods might call off the hunt. The warriors would take the body take to the village for a proper send-off to the spirit realm, and to sit in council to select a new leader. That would take time, precious time he could use to get Susan to safety.

The six riders were scanning the ground, evidently seeking tracks.

Fargo glanced up at the canopy of limbs overhead. This time he didn't need to worry about the sun, and they wouldn't be able to charge him because he wasn't about to open fire until they were so close he could see the sweat on their brows. He braced his left shoulder against the tree and waited.

On they came, until they were forty yards away. Then they halted and a discussion started between Blue Raven and Iron Tail. From the hand motions and the pointing they did, they were arguing over whether to continue along the stream or search in another direction.

Fargo peeked out at them, his thumb stroking the hammer in anticipation. Suddenly, to his rear, came the muffled crunch of stealthy footfalls. He spun, leveling the rifle, thinking there had been other Bloods nearby that he hadn't seen.

A few yards away, Susan halted and protectively raised her hands in front of her face as if to ward off a bullet. "It's me!" she blurted in consternation.

Fargo glanced at Blue Raven and the Bloods, who were still talking. "I can see that," he snapped, lowering the Sharps. He stepped to her side, gripped her left forearm and hauled her a dozen feet into the undergrowth.

"You're hurting me," she whined, trying to yank her arm loose.

Fargo let go and angrily jabbed her chest with a finger.

"What the hell do you think you're doing? Are you trying to get both of us killed?"

"I didn't want to stay back there by myself," Susan replied testily, raising her voice.

"Keep quiet," Fargo warned, "unless you want Blue Raven to know we're here."

"Blue Raven?"

Fargo jerked his thumb toward the riders. "Didn't you see them?"

Her eyes narrowed as she gazed through the brush, then widened in dismay. "Oh my God. No, I didn't know they were there."

"You nearly blundered into the open and gave us away," Fargo said softly. "Now I want you to sneak back to the horses and wait there for me."

"No."

"This isn't the time to be arguing."

"I won't wait there alone," Susan stubbornly objected. "I'd rather stay with you."

"It's too dangerous, damn it," Fargo said. "You might be hit by a wild shot."

Susan crossed her arms and stamped her right foot. "I'm not leaving," she whispered, "and that's final."

Fuming, about to give her a shove to start her on her way, Fargo looked toward the grassland and saw with a start that Blue Raven and the warriors were approaching. "Get down," he directed and ran back to the tree, keeping low. Warily, he peeked out.

Blue Raven and Iron Tail were in the lead, side by side. The four Bloods behind them were bunched together. Only the renegade carried a rifle; the rest had bows, and none had arrows nocked to their strings.

Fargo stared at Blue Raven, bothered by something he couldn't put his finger on. In the back of his mind a small voice seemed to be hinting that he was missing a crucial fact. He didn't realize his intuition was right until the riders were twenty-five yards away and he recognized the rifle in Blue Raven's hands as being a Sharps.

Not that the big rifle would do Blue Raven much good. Fargo guessed the renegade had taken it from the man slain near the lake. Unless Blue Raven had owned one once before, he could hardly be an expert with the gun already. At long range he wouldn't be much of a threat, and at short range a Sharps only had one advantage over other rifles and pistols: more stopping power.

Fargo heard their voices, heard Blue Raven and the chief talking in the Blood tongue. Iron Tail was riding close to the water's edge, which left Blue Raven a perfect target.

Just to play it safe, Skye eased down and pulled the Arkansas toothpick from his boot. He wedged the knife under his belt to use in case he expended all the rounds in his guns and still hadn't finished off his foes.

One of the Bloods had twisted to survey the surrounding mountains.

Fargo pulled his head from view and checked on Susan, who was kneeling behind a bush. Then he gazed at the stream, waiting for the riders to come into his line of vision. Their shadows materialized first, outlandish black shapes dancing on the bank, and seconds later both the chief and Blue Raven appeared. Not yet, Fargo had to remind himself. Wait for all of them.

Two of the Bloods were next.

Now the last two, Fargo thought, and noticed Blue Raven idly glanced in his direction, straight at the tree against which his profile could easily be distinguished. He saw recognition sprout in the renegade's eyes. Blue Raven cried out and started to bring his rifle to bear.

Got you, Fargo thought grimly. He snapped his Sharps to his shoulder, taking an instant bead on the center of Blue Raven's forehead. He fired, his slug spraying blood and brains from the rear of Blue Raven's cranium and smacking the renegade from the saddle.

Dropping the Sharps with his left hand, Fargo simultaneously drew his Colt with the right, taking a step out from the tree as he did. The .44 boomed and Iron Tail was hurled from his horses to splash down in the stream.

The next two Bloods' arms streaked from their quivers to their bow strings, frantically trying to get arrows nocked on their bows. Behind them, the final pair had a different idea.

Even as Iron Tail went down, they whipped their horses toward the big man in the white hat.

Fargo stood firm and squeezed off two more shots, knowing he must make each count. At the blasting of his Colt, the two warriors striving to empty bows were both shot in the head. Both promptly fell, leaving only the pair who were charging him.

Pivoting, Fargo had to tilt the Colt upward, so close were the onrushing braves. He nailed the warrior on the right, sending a slug into the man's chest that knocked the Blood off the rear of his mount. The last Indian, though, was almost upon him, in the act of drawing the bow string back to his chest.

Fargo back-pedaled, raising the .44 to go for a chest shot. He had the Blood dead to rights in his sights when his right heel caught on an exposed root. Fargo stumbled, falling to one knee, giving the Blood time to get right on top of him. He looked up and saw the hate-filled face of the bloodthirsty warrior, the arrow tip aiming directly at his head.

19

From Fargo's rear arose a terrified shriek, an ear-piercing scream that distracted the charging Blood at the very moment he was about to loose the shaft, causing him to glance toward the source. In the blink of an eye, Fargo had the Colt centered and fired.

At the selfsame instant the Blood released the arrow.

Fargo saw the barbed tip leap toward him. He recoiled, unable to do anything else before it reached him, feeling the feathers brush his hair as the shaft streaked past, the point missing his ear by the width of a hair.

The last Blood rode eight more feet, swaying wildly, his hands clutching his chest, then crashed to the ground. He landed in a thorny thicket, thrashed for a bit and was still.

Rising, Fargo scanned the bodies. Not a one was moving. He looked over his shoulder at Susan, who had risen, her mouth still open from her yell. "Thanks," he said.

She nodded meekly, gulped and came over. 'I thought you were a goner."

"That makes two of us."

Susan stared at Blue Raven, who was sprawled on his back, his black eyes fixed on the empty sky. Her cheeks tinged with red, she glanced at the knife under Fargo's belt. "May I?" she asked, extending her right hand.

"You want my knife?" Fargo asked, surprised by the request.

"Yes. Please."

"Why? They're all dead."

"Please, Skye," Susan said, her eyes pleading with him, her fingers trembling.

Fargo slowly pulled the throwing knife out and placed the hilt in her palm. "Be careful with that. It's razor sharp."

"I hope so," she responded, and walked with measured steps over to where Blue Raven lay. Stopping on his left side, near his waist, she slowly bent her legs and knelt. A few tears rolled down her cheeks and her lower lip quivered from the intensity of her emotions.

In a burst of insight Fargo deduced what was coming. He took a hasty stride toward her, horrified by the realization, but he was too late.

Susan swept the knife aloft, shuddered, and drove the keen point into Blue Raven's groin.

Fargo stopped, appalled, seeing blood appear where the knife hilt rested in the renegade's pants. "Susan—" he said, but she didn't hear him, or if she did, she ignored him because again she raised the knife and plunged it all the way into Blue Raven's privates. "Don't do this to yourself."

"I must," Susan choked out and then repeated, almost in a whisper, "I must." The tears flowed from her in earnest now, and her body shook as she stabbed Blue Raven again and again and again.

The sight gave Fargo the shivers.

They reached the pass north of the pond late the next afternoon, having ridden their stallions to near exhaustion and successfully evaded yet another band of Bloods along the way.

Fargo took the lead, anxious to learn if Calhoun and Badger Woman were all right. At the end of the pass he reined up, scouring the forest to the east of the pond. There was no trace of smoke, nothing to indicate his friends were still there. He went down the incline to the tree line and cupped his hands to his mouth. "Wes! Are you here?"

Almost immediately there was a whoop of elation, and from deep in the forest came Calhoun's reply. "I sure am, pardner. Be right there."

"He sounds happy that you're back," Susan commented.

"Only because he's not very fond of grizzly bears," Fargo said and heard the crackling of underbrush as his friend hastened toward him.

Calhoun appeared from between two trees, astride one horse and leading another. He beamed, riding up and looking at Susan Chambers. "He did it! The son of a bitch did it! You're okay?"

"Yes, I am," Susan said rather formally. "Thank you for your concern, Mr. Calhoun."

The gambler moved his horse next to the Ovaro and clapped the Trailsman on the back. "It's great to see you again. I was getting lonely with just crickets for company."

Fargo looked at the forest. "Where's Badger Woman?"

"She left," Calhoun said. "I tried to talk her out of the notion, but the little lady was as stubborn as a Missouri mule."

"Where did she go?" Fargo asked, surprised at the news.

"She said she knew where another Shoshoni village is located, about eight miles east of here," Calhoun disclosed. "She told me that she could get there by herself, that she didn't need my help. She wanted to hurry because she was afraid the village would be moved before she got there. I gave her the other horse so she wouldn't have to walk the whole way."

"When was this?"

"This morning," Calhoun said. "She asked me to say good-bye for her. Claimed you would understand."

Fargo shrugged. "Who can understand women?"

Calhoun laughed, then saw Susan giving both of them a stern scrutiny. He cleared his throat and commented, "I reckon women do."

"So what now?" Susan inquired. "Do we push on until dark?"

The big man squinted up at the sun, which hung above the western horizon. "No. We'll make camp here for the night. There's plenty of feed and water for the horses, and our stallions need some rest. Tomorrow we'll start out bright and early."

"Fine with me," Calhoun said. "I can't wait to get back to civilization."

"What about your little problem?" Fargo asked.

"I face up to them and finish it one way or the other," Calhoun stated.

"What problem is this?" Susan wanted to know.

"It's personal, ma'am," Calhoun answered, fiddling with the brim of his hat. "Not a topic for a lady." He promptly swung down and headed toward the pond. "I reckon we'd better get started on making camp."

Fargo saw Susan give the gambler a curious look and knew Calhoun would be pestered with questions before the night was done. Arousing a woman's curiosity and then not providing the answers she needed was akin to trying to douse a raging fire by throwing kindling on it. Calhoun had unwittingly fanned an inferno. "We'll camp where we did the first night," he said to the gambler. "I'll take care of finding something to eat."

"Better you than me," Calhoun replied. "I'm not partial to eating pine needles."

Grinning, Fargo dismounted.

Between the three of them they quickly prepared for bedding down. Calhoun took care of watering the mounts. Susan volunteered to start the fire. And Fargo went into the forest and used his throwing knife to kill two large rabbits. After the critters were skinned and roasting on a spit, the three of them settled back and made small talk.

Fargo noticed that Susan seemed especially interested in Calhoun. She exercised her feminine wiles cleverly, and before an hour had passed she had the gambler eating out of her hand. They wound up sitting next to each other and talking in soft tones. Fargo wasn't offended in the least. He knew he'd be riding on as soon as she was delivered safely to the wagon train. By the time he settled down on his blanket to go to sleep, the two of them were whispering and showing more teeth than a litter of beavers. He fell asleep listening to the friendly drone of their voices.

Next morning at the crack of dawn he was up. Calhoun was snoring on the far side of the smoldering fire while Susan slept soundly halfway between the two of them. He watered the horses and got the fire blazing again before waking them, starting with the gambler.

Calhoun sat up the instant Fargo laid a hand on him. He looked around, blinked, and grinned. "Thank goodness it's just you. For a second there I thought I was being jumped by renegades."

"Blue Raven's bunch is finished. We don't have to worry about them any more," Fargo said and moved over to Susan to gently shake her shoulder. She took longer to awaken, and when her lovely eyes flicked wide they held a hint of confusion, as if she didn't quite know where she was. "Good morning," Fargo said.

"Oh. Skye. I was having the most horrible dream," Susan said, pressing a palm to her smooth forehead. "I dreamt I was being chased by a headless man dressed just like Blue Raven."

"I told you before. Try to forget about him."

"I'm doing my best."

Fargo prepared coffee while the other two attended to arranging their clothes and paying the undergrowth a visit. The hot liquid tasted delicious and he savored the tangy fragrance while admiring the sunrise, the striking hues of scarlet, orange, and pink filling the eastern sky.

In half an hour they were in the saddle and heading south, Calhoun leading the spare animal. Little was said as they traversed the rough terrain, constantly alert for Indians and wild beasts. Twice they spied grizzlies, but fortunately the big bears were foraging off in the distance and didn't attack. At midday they halted beside a spring to give the horses a rest.

Fargo had noticed Susan gazing at Calhoun a lot during the morning, and he figured she had designs on the gambler. So he wasn't surprised when he heard her ask a question that caused Calhoun's eyebrows to arch upward.

"Have you ever thought of doing something other than making a living at a card table?"

"Who, me?"

"No, I'm talking to that horse over there," Susan said, pointing at her stallion.

"I like gambling," Calhoun told her. "If my luck holds, I'll do it the rest of my life."

"What about having a family and a home?"

"I've never given them much thought," Calhoun said. "Maybe I will when I'm ready to grow roots, which is still a long way off."

"It must be lonely living your kind of life," Susan said.

"I've never noticed."

"You will, sooner or later, and then you'll regret not

having married a good woman when you had the chance."

Fargo almost laughed at the comical expression on Calhoun's face as the gambler pondered her words. He almost hated to announce, "I reckon it's time to hit the trail."

Onward they rode, traveling until evening when they made camp in a narrow gully where they were sheltered from the high wind and their fire would avoid detection by hostile eyes. Fargo killed several quail for their meal, which Susan roasted. Eventually all three of them turned in.

The next two days were spent much like the first and by late afternoon of the third day, a wide ribbon of water appeared ahead.

"What's that?" Susan asked.

"The Green River," Fargo said. "We'll follow it quite a spell, then cut across to Absaroka Ridge. By tomorrow afternoon, or thereabouts, you'll be back with your pa."

Susan squealed in delight. "I can hardly wait."

"If we ride all night, we'll get there that much faster," Calhoun said.

"We've already pushed the horses hard enough for one day," Fargo said. "After coming so far, one more night won't make much of a difference."

"Maybe not to you," Susan said.

They made camp one final time on the east shore of the Green River. Susan became silent and moody at the prospect of the impending reunion with her father. Calhoun spent a lot of time secretly looking at her. Fargo tended the fire and tried not to laugh.

Another gorgeous sunrise greeted them the next morning. Excited about going back to her family. Susan was the first up. She rustled the others out of their blankets and in twenty minutes they were underway.

Fargo took the lead, sticking to the bank, moving at a rapid pace. He was quite eager to get the pair to the wagons, then take off. Long before he came to the spot where he'd slain the grizzly, he saw a few buzzards flapping ponderously into the air. He glimpsed the rotted carcass from a distance and decided to swing around it to spare Susan the ugly sight.

Soon they were back along the river, the murky water

flowing sluggishly on their right, green forest on their left. Fargo was relaxed, sitting loosely in the saddle, idly surveying the landscape ahead.

"Do you reckon the troopers from Fort Laramie have got there by now?" Calhoun asked.

"I figure it will be another day or two," Fargo answered, glad the soldiers were coming. It would relieve him of any responsibility to linger should Webber or anyone else ask him to do so.

A broad stretch of flat, sandy ground stretched out before them, an area where the Green River periodically overflowed during the annual spring runoff from the high peaks to the north. The high waters had formed a sheer bank on the left, six feet in height at the rim, which was overgrown with weeds and dotted with rocks.

Fargo stayed near the bank. He knew the soil closer to the water could be treacherous—soft and pocked with small sink holes that would cause his horse to stumble or worse. Concentrating on the ground, he was taken unawares by the harsh bellow from the bank at his elbow.

"Rein up or die!"

20

Fargo glanced around and instantly stopped at the sight of two rifles and a pistol trained on all three of them. He recognized the hardcases holding the guns right away—Dell and Tick Bowdrie, and Pony Banner. Behind him Susan gasped and Calhoun must have made a move for his revolver, because Dell Bowdrie tensed, extended the Colt he held, and growled a warning. "Go ahead, gambler man. I'd as soon kill you now as later."

All three were braced to fire. Fargo hoped Calhoun wouldn't do anything rash. He saw the trio relax and knew the gambler had decided against a foolish play.

"Smart man," Dell taunted Calhoun. He wagged his Colt. "Now I want the three of you to sit right still while Pony collects your hardware. Not one move, you hear?"

Banner started to slide down the bank, using his rifle stock as a crutch to keep himself upright.

"Who are you men?" Susan demanded angrily. "What do you want? Why are you doing this?"

"You must be the Chambers gal we were told about," Dell Bowdrie said, touching his hand to his hat brim. "My apologies for the inconvenience, but we have business with Calhoun and Fargo. Once that's taken care of, we'll see to it that you get back to the wagon train."

"What kind of business?" Susan asked.

Fargo kept his eyes on Pony Banner as the man walked over and took the Sharps and his .44. Then Banner walked toward the gambler. He held himself still, knowing the Bowdrie brothers would cut loose if he didn't.

"Our business concerns our brother, Frank," Dell was saying. "You see, ma'am, Wes Calhoun murdered him."

"It was a fair fight," Calhoun snapped.

"There's fair, and then there's fair," Dell responded testily. "Frank wasn't no gunman. He was no match for you. So it was murder, plain and simple."

Tick Bowdrie snickered and hefted his rifle. "Should I plug him now, Dell?"

"And spoil all our fun? No, you idiot. First things first."

Fargo saw Banner return with Calhoun's revolver, adding to the collection that the thin man desposited at the base of the bank. Straightening, Banner swung around and raised his own rifle.

"I've got them covered, Dell. Come on down."

Both Bowdries dug in their boot heels at the edge of the rim and slid down to the bottom. Tick nearly fell on his face.

"Now we can get started," Dell declared with a sadistic smirk. "Climb off those critters and be quick about it."

With no other choice, Fargo swung down, careful to keep his hands in the open. He didn't want to provoke them before it came time to make his play. Of the three, he rated Tick as the most dangerous simply because the younger Bowdrie appeared to be as tightly strung as a piano wire and liable to snap at any sound. Not that Dell or Pony Banner were any less deadly, but they would take a hair longer to react to any threat.

Susan took a step toward Dell, her fists tight at her sides. "I want you to know I resent this treatment, and you can be sure I'll tell the troopers from Fort Laramie when they reach the wagon train."

"I wouldn't be talking like that if I was you," Dell said.

Fargo wanted to motion her to be quiet, but Tick was glaring at him, ready to shoot.

"Why not?" Susan snapped. "I can say what I want."

Dell bowed his head, thinking, then looked at his brother. "I reckon we'll make it three."

"Can I do her?" Tick asked eagerly.

Susan glanced from one to the other. "What do you mean?" she inquired. "Surely you wouldn't harm a woman?"

"When that woman might spill the beans to the army, I reckon we don't have much choice but to fix her hash permanentlike," Dell said and his brother laughed. "You should have kept your lips sealed, little lady."

Calhoun, who had been holding himself rock still, his eyes

simmering with indignation, said, "Leave her out of this affair. Only a coward kills someone who can't fight back."

"Did I ask your opinion?" Dell Bowdrie demanded and walked up to the gambler. Before anyone could guess his intent, he brought his revolver up and around, the barrel striking Calhoun on the temple.

Fargo almost took a step to help when Calhoun dropped to his knees, clutching his head, but Tick and Banner both had their weapons fixed on him. He slowly elevated his arms, pretending to be cowed but tensed his legs in readiness for a leap.

Dell Bowdrie shoved Calhoun to the ground. "The little lady isn't the only one who doesn't know when to keep her mouth shut, is she?" He hauled off and kicked Calhoun in the side, causing the gamblelr to double in half in acute pain.

"Leave him alone!" Susan cried and threw herself at Dell, her fists beating ineffectively on his brawny arms. He looked at her in surprise, then down at Calhoun. Finally he gave her a casual shove that nonetheless drove her back over four feet. "Ain't this interesting," he said.

"What is?" Tick asked.

"The way this filly is sticking up for the gambler man," Dell said. "It makes a fella wonder."

Tick's forehead knit as he attempted to think, his gaze straying to Susan and Calhoun. Suddenly he smiled. "I get it, big brother. You reckon she's giving him some?"

"Appears so."

"She not giving him anything," Fargo came to her defense, dreading what the trio would do if they pegged Susan as a loose woman. "They're just friends."

"Is that a fact?" Dell responded sarcastically. "They won't be friends for much longer, though." He chuckled, holstered his Colt, and leaned down to haul Calhoun into a sitting position. "Now that's much better."

Pony Banner gestured with his rifle at Fargo. "Shouldn't we tie this big bastard up if you're going to start work on the gambler?"

Dell looked up. "Yep. Tie them both. I don't want the filly kicking up her heels when the blood gets to flowing."

"All right, mister," Banner said, aiming at Fargo's midsection. "Turn around and put your hands behind your back. You too, lady."

Frowning, Fargo complied, watching Susan also turn.

"Want me to go fetch a lasso from one of our horses?" Tick asked Banner.

"No need," the thin hardcase replied. "I've got some lash rope in my pocket here."

Fargo's hopes rose a mite. Lash rope was the kind used to secure packs of animals. It wasn't as thick as a lasso and would be slightly easier to cut, provided he could get to his throwing knife. He felt a hand press his wrists together, and then lash rope was looped four times around his wrists and a knot was tied.

"That ought to do it," Pony Banner stated.

Glancing over his shoulder, Fargo observed the thin killer bind Susan, tying her in the exact same way. Then, hearing a thud, he faced front where Dell Bowdrie had knocked Calhoun down again.

"You men are despicable!" Susan cried.

"If you don't shut your mouth, you'll lose some teeth," Dell warned her, and nodded at Pony Banner. "Get them off their feet and we can commence breaking every bone in Calhoun's body."

Banner placed his hands on Susan's shoulders and forced her to sit on the ground, then turned to Fargo. "You know what to do, mister, so do it unless you want your knees shot out from under you."

Skye slowly knelt and waited to see if the hardcases would insist that he sit down all the way. To his relief, they didn't. Now his hands were within inches of his boots. Unfortunately, Tick Bowdrie and Pony Banner were standing to his rear. If he attempted to slide the knife out, they'd know.

Dell Bowdrie placed his brawny hands on his hips and stood over Calhoun. "Tick, go fetch the horses. I have an idea how we can have us a little fun before we finish this hombre off."

"On my way," Tick said. Spinning, he began climbing the bank.

Talk about a tight spot, Fargo reflected. If he didn't get

loose soon, Calhoun would windup dead. The gambler was lying on his left side, bent at the waist, wheezing from the second kick.

"I hope you won't drag this out like you did the last time," Banner said to Dell.

"What's the matter? Got a case of the jitters?"

The thin hardcase anxiously surveyed the landscape. "This is Indian country. I don't like the notion of being interrupted by a band of Sioux or Utes."

"You fret too damn much," Dell said. "And I'm not about to rush after all the trouble we've gone to tracking this son of a bitch down." He jabbed the tip of his boot into Calhoun's back and Calhoun grunted.

Fargo winced, burning with anger. "How did you know we would be coming this way?" he asked, hoping to spare his friend a little grief by distracting the older Bowdrie.

Dell chuckled. "Now that was right slick, if I do say so myself. We were watching when you left the wagon train, and we saw which way you headed. Then we took our leave, telling those good folks that we were going back to Fort Laramie. We rode in that direction for a ways, until we were sure they couldn't see us, then we circled around and found your trail. We're not much at tracking, but yours was easy to spot, what with you leading all those extra critters."

Pony Banner laughed and stepped between Fargo and Susan. "Tell him my idea, Dell."

"Don't rush me," Dell snapped. He nodded at the Green River. "We found where you had stuck to the river and followed your sign for quite a ways. Then Pony had a brainstorm. Instead of going to all the trouble of trying to trail you without being seen and risk having that Sharps of yours used on us, he figured we could wait right here until Calhoun or you showed up."

"Pretty clever, huh?" Banner said.

"You're a bright one," Fargo responded dryly, annoyed at himself for assuming they would leave him alone for a while after the way he had humiliated them at the wagon train. A man who assumed too much about his enemies usually wound up six feet under.

"To tell the truth," Dell went on, "I was about ready to

chuck it in and leave when you showed up. Real thoughtful of you.'' He tossed back his head and roared.

Fargo glanced at Banner, who had picked up his rifle again after tying their arms and now held the weapon at an angle, the barrel within inches of Susan's temple. He noticed Calhoun look toward her and frown.

"Where the hell is that no account brother of mine?" Dell demanded, pivoting toward the bank. "He must of went all the way to Missouri for those horses."

The next moment Tick appeared to the south, leading the three mounts. He was searching the bank and apparently found what he wanted—a section where the slope wasn't as steep—then brought the animals to the bottom. "Here they are," he announced as he approached.

"About damn time, you lunkhead," Dell said. "Get one of the lassos and tie it to the gambler's ankles."

"You bet."

Fargo stiffened, aware of what Dell had in mind. And he still couldn't go for the knife, not with Banner hovering beside him.

"What are you fixing to do?" Susan demanded.

"Have us some fun," Dell answered. "We're going to find out just how tough this gambler is."

"Bastards!"

Dell made a clucking sound with his tongue. "What a mouth for a lady," he baited her.

Carrying a lasso, Tick walked to Calhoun, drew his revolver and motioned for Calhoun to roll onto his back. Glaring, the gambler obeyed and Tick quickly wrapped one end of the rope around Calhoun's ankles and tied a big knot to hold it securely in place. "There we go, big brother," he said, standing.

Dell took the other end of the rope and walked to one of the horses, a big bay. He began tying the rope to the saddle horn. "I've always wanted to know how long a man can hold his breath," he remarked.

Susan glanced at the river, then at Calhoun. "You wouldn't!" she exclaimed, aghast.

"Watch me," Dell said.

Fargo decided to take a gamble. Inching his fingers to the

bottom of his right leg, he slipped his fingers into his boot and just touched the knife hilt when Tick gazed in his direction. He froze, hoping Banner wouldn't look down.

"How about if I hog-tie Fargo and haul him around?" Tick proposed.

"One at a time," Dell replied. "You two can guard them and keep watch for Indians while I teach Calhoun why no one with half a brain tangles with the Bowdrie clan."

"Aw, shucks," Tick said.

"You'll get your turn next," Dell promised and swung into the saddle.

Fargo eased his fingers in farther, his shoulders straining, trying to keep the rest of his body still so as not to alert the hardcases. He saw Calhoun sit up and places his left hand on the inside of his right forearm, as if he was in pain.

"You all set, gambler man?" Dell asked.

"Go to hell," Calhoun answered.

"Maybe I will one day," Dell said, "but you're going first." He spurred the bay forward, the rope losing its slack as the horse went faster and faster, and a second later Calhoun's legs were jerked straight and he was dragged over the rough ground at breakneck speed.

21

"No!" Susan screamed in terror.

Dell Bowdrie laughed wickedly as he brought the bay to a full gallop, gazing over his left shoulder at the man he planned to kill in a slow, acutely painful fashion. He angled along the shore within inches of the water's edge.

"Make him suffer, Dell!" Tick called out, his face flushed with excitement. He took several strides to get a better view. Pony Banner joined him.

Calhoun was flat on his back, his body swaying with the motion of the lasso and bouncing whenever he hit a bump or a rut. He held his forearms pressed tight to his chest. In the first few seconds his black hat flew off and his frock coat hitched up around his shoulders, cushioning them slightly from the rough ground.

Fargo had the opening he needed. Neither Tick nor Pony were paying any attention to him. He yanked the throwing knife, reversed his grip on the hilt by carefully twirling the weapon with his fingers and glanced back to align the razor edge on top of the lash rope. Sawing methodically, he went to work on the bindings while watching Dell Bowdrie, afraid the hardcase would deliberately ride Calhoun over rocks or into a boulder. Instead, seconds later, Dell cut his horse into the Green River.

Susan screamed again, only louder. "Don't!" she shrieked. "You'll kill him!"

"That's the general idea, woman," Tick responded sarcastically without bothering to look at her.

Calhoun went in feet first, his back bowed as he attempted to keep his mouth above the surface. The water sprayed back over his face and hair, instantly drenching him. Oddly, he didn't bother using his arms in any way; he simply held them close to his chest.

What in tarnation was the gambler doing? Fargo wondered and glanced back to check his progress. Every loop had been partially cut, and a few more strokes should do the trick. With Tick and Pony preoccupied, it should be easy.

Susan cried out, "Stop, damn you! You're killing him!" She rose, grunting with the effort, and ran toward the river. "Stop tormenting him!"

Fargo imitated a rock, concerned that the other two hard-cases would turn and see his movement.

Both Tick and Pony Banner whirled to intercept her. They each took hold of her arm and held her securely, refusing to let go even though she kicked and jerked from side to side.

"Quit fighting, you hellcat," Tick snapped. "You're only making it harder on yourself."

The bay reached the far bank and Dell turned, not even bothering to go up on land. He hollered in sadistic delight as he headed back.

Fargo could barely see Calhoun's head above the water. The gambler was gasping, his head twisted to one side in a futile bid to avoid the water rippling up over his chest over his face. At the rate Calhoun was going, he wouldn't last long. With renewed urgency, Fargo attacked the lash ropes. He felt one part, then another, and after one more stroke the bindings fell away and his hands were free.

Now he had another problem. If he tried to slay Tick and Banner while they were holding Susan, she might wind up hurt or worse. He had to bide his time. But if he did, then Calhoun would be the one who died. No matter what he did, he'd lose a friend. He was caught between a rock and a hard place.

Dell Bowdrie was slowing down near the center of the river, cackling as Calhoun floundered, sank, and sputtererd above the surface again and again. "What's the matter, gambler man?" he shouted. "Where's the ace up your sleeve now?"

"You animals!" Susan declared, and landed a solid kick on Tick Bowdrie's right shin. "You filthy animals!"

Grimacing in pain, Tick suddenly let go of her arm and backhanded her across the mouth, the blow tearing her from Banner's grasp and causing her to fall at their feet. "You bitch!" he roared. "I ought to kick your fool head in."

"You do and your brother will have your hide," Banner warned him. "Be patient. You'll get your turn."

"I ain't a patient man," Tick stated.

"Don't I know it," Banner responded irritably.

Fargo tensed his legs for the leap he must make, his right hand grasping the knife hilt. Out in the water, Dell had goaded the bay into a gallop again, laughing as the powerful horse dragged Calhoun the rest of the way to the shore. Since Dell was now facing forward, Fargo paused, knowing the killer would shout a warning to the others if he made his bid.

"This is the most fun I've had in a coon's age," Dell stated as he rode out of the water, clear up to his brother and Banner. By then Calhoun was also on land, on his left side, sputtering and wheezing and sucking precious air into his strained lungs.

"When do I get to drag someone?" Tick asked eagerly.

"Just wait your turn," Dell chided him, and dismounted. He hitched at his gunbelt and walked toward the gambler. "You won't die on me yet, I hope. I have a real treat in store for you."

"Leave him alone!" Susan wailed, trying to stand.

Tick stared at her in disgust. "You never learn," he said, and kicked her in the stomach, flattening her. "Now keep that contrary mouth of yours closed or the next time you'll eat boot leather."

Fargo placed his hands on the ground, ready to spring. He knew Dell would likely nail him even if he killed the other two, but he had to make the attempt.

The older Bowdrie was less than six feet from Calhoun, who was on his side, his arms clasped to his shirt, huffing and puffing. "Got your wind yet?" he mocked his victim. "I hope so. I'm ready to commence skinning you alive."

"Like hell you will," Calhoun replied, not even looking at his tormentor.

Dell snickered. "And what's to stop me?"

"That ace up my sleeve," Calhoun said and uncoiled with the speed of a striking rattler, his right hand sweeping up and out toward Dell Bowdrie. Clutched in his fingers, glistening in the sunlight, was a derringer.

Dell halted in shock, then made a belated try for his hog-leg.

The derringer cracked once.

Struck in the temple, Dell spun halfway around, a red hole marking the entry point, his face scrunched up in ludicrous amazement at his fate. His right hand tugged feebly at his revolver, but went limp before the gun cleared leather. Staggering, he walked a few steps toward his brother, then pitched on his face.

"No!" Tick shrieked, and went for his own revolver.

In a rush Fargo was up and bounding toward the two men, vaulting into the air just as Tick brought his six-shooter out. He slammed into the middle of Tick's back, knocking him forward, causing the killer to trip over Susan and fall to the ground as the gun blasted. The slug tore harmlessly into the earth instead of Wes Calhoun.

Fargo came down on his right side, narrowly missing Susan, and rolled to his knees. Already Pony Banner was trying to bring his rifle to bear. Whipping his right arm back, then straight ahead, Fargo sent the throwing knife into Banner's chest and heard the clear thud as the weapon hit home.

Stumbling back, Banner let go of the rifle and grabbed at the knife hilt, his eyes wide in shock. He tugged futilely for a moment, then sagged, his legs giving out from under him. Blood spurted from the left corner of his mouth.

Fargo twisted and saw Tick rising a few feet away with rabid hatred lining his features. He sprang before Tick could fire. His left hand clamped on Tick's right wrist, holding the gun barrel at bay, while his right streaked to Tick's throat and squeezed.

Despite his short stature, Tick Bowdrie was possessed of the strength of a madman. He rammed his left fist into Skye's gut twice, then connected on the chin.

Stars exploded before Fargo's eyes. He threw himself to the right, taking Tick with him, not relinquishing his grip on the gun hand for a second. They landed on their sides and he drew back his leg to knee Tick in the groin.

The younger Bowdrie beat him to it, hissing as his right knee arced into Fargo's privates.

A wave of sheer agony washed over Fargo. Momentary weakness seized him. Before he could hope to prevent it, Tick wrenched himself free and scrambled backward. Fargo saw the hardcase's gun hand rising, aware with dreadful certainty a bullet would rip through his body the very next instant. In desperation he flung his legs out, connecting with both boots on Tick's chest and slamming Tick into his back. The revolver sailed to one side.

Fargo rose in a crouch, saw Tick do the same and make for the gun. He leaped, tackling Tick around the knees and bringing both of them down once again. He rained a flurry of blows on Tick's head and chest. Then they grappled and rolled—first one way, then another—neither gaining a distinct advantage.

Fargo wound up on his back. Tick lifted a fist high to strike him in the face, but this time Fargo beat him to the punch and smashed the man's nostrils with one blow of his own brawny hand. A second blow downed Tick in a heap on Fargo's legs, and he kicked the unconscious killer off.

"You did it!" Susan screeched, elated. "You did it!"

Nodding, wishing his privates would stop pulsating with throbbing anguish, Fargo pushed to his feet and wobbled unsteadily.

"Are you all right?" Susan inquired.

"Never felt better," Fargo muttered, glancing at Calhoun. The gambler was sitting up, breathing better now, the derringer still extended.

"I couldn't get a clear shot," Calhoun said, managing a lopsided grin. "Your big head kept getting in the way."

"Don't blame me if you can't aim worth a hoot," Fargo retorted. He shuffled to Susan's side to untie her and knelt. "Are you okay?"

She gave him a fond look. "Yes, thanks to you. You seem to be making a habit out of saving my life."

"Thank Wes. He gave me the opening I needed to pull it off."

"I reckon I will. Later," Susan said and gazed at the gambler in unstinted admiration, her feelings obvious.

Fargo was having a hard time undoing the knots Banner had made; they were too tight. He glanced at the dead man, saw his knife jutting from Banner's chest and moved past Susan to reclaim it. As he did, she abruptly cried out in alarm.

"Skye! Behind you!"

Fargo didn't need to look to know the reason. He saw Pony Banner's rifle lying cocked near his boots and swept down, picking up the gun, even as he pivoted on his heels to see Tick Bowdrie, revolver in hand, taking aim. Fargo didn't bother raising the rifle to his shoulder. He merely leveled the weapon and squeezed the trigger.

At the booming report Tick was picked up and hurled over four feet to come down with a loud thud on his back. He gamely tried to rise yet again, his gun arm waving sluggishly. A lingering exhale marked his last breath and with a convulsive jerking of both legs, he died.

"Looks like we're even," Fargo said to Susan, tossing the rifle aside.

"Did you ever think of becoming a marshal?" she asked.

"No," Fargo replied, surprised by the question. "Why?"

Susan glanced at the Bowdries and Pony Banner, thoughtfully regarding each body and said softly, "I think you have a knack for that kind of work."

It was early the next afternoon when Fargo spied the wagons near Absaroka Ridge and noticed smoke curling skyward from a dozen cooking fires. He reined up, and his companions followed his example.

"What's wrong?" Susan asked. "Why are you stopping?"

"This is as far as I go."

Susan and Calhoun exchanged puzzled expressions.

"Why not go all the way?" the gambler inquired. "I reckon her pa would like to thank you for all you've done."

Fargo thought of Gretchen—of warm, fun-loving, lovely Gretchen—who would be awaiting his return so she could invite him to her wagon again, bed him again, and try to persuade him to stay with her—again. His manhood tingled at the memory of his last visit, and he shook his head to clear his mind.

"Are you sure you're all right?" Susan asked.

"Fine," Fargo said, smiling at her. "You two go on. Your pa will be overjoyed to have you back safe and sound."

"This doesn't seem right, somehow," she said.

"I have business elsewhere," Fargo said and looked at the gambler. "What about you, Wes? Are you heading back East?"

Calhoun glanced at Susan, then at the wagons. "I don't rightly know. I may just head on out Oregon way after all. Maybe there's more out there for a man like me than I figured."

"You never know," Fargo said, suppressing a grin. He went to goad the Ovaro into motion.

"Wait!" Susan urged. She moved her horse beside his and leaned over to give him a hug. "I'll never forget you," she promised, her cheek on his chest, her voice strained. "For as long as I live, you'll always have a special place in my heart."

Fargo squeezed her back, then gave her a peck on the top of her head. "You take care of yourself. Find the right man and raise that family you want. And always remember to hold your head up proud. You're a damn fine woman, Susan Chambers."

She drew back, tears flowing down her cheeks, and coughed. "Thank you." She paused. "Is there anything we can say to change your mind?"

"I reckon not," Fargo said and offered his hand to Calhoun. They shook, their eyes conveying their friendship, and then he gripped the reins and rode eastward, turning his back on the wagon train and Gretchen Rice—on security and the seductive charms of a woman who wanted to tie him to her skirts—to return to the untamed land and the unfettered freedom he loved as much as life itself.

LOOKING FORWARD!

**The following is the opening
section from the next novel in the exciting
Trailsman series from Signet:**

THE TRAILSMAN #121
REDWOOD REVENGE

*1860, the fiercely rugged land
of the West Montana Territory,
where the only law was the one
men made for themselves. . . .*

Nobody wants to be shot dead.

Not anywhere, not anyway, not anytime.

But being shot dead in bed is the worst of all, especially in the middle of enjoying a warm and willing woman. It not only robs a man of his life, it robs him of his dignity, as well. It adds insult to injury.

These thoughts had exploded through Fargo's mind as shots thudded into the bed, flashes of philosophy as unwanted and ill-timed as the sound of the bullets. And now they returned to him once again as he sat beneath the narrowleaf cottonwood, glad to be alive and filled with anger at how it had all turned out. This was his first chance to let his mind unreel and he decided to go back over everything that had happened, step-by-step and piece by piece.

He'd start at the beginning—his arrival in town—that suddenly seemed a lot longer than a half-dozen hours ago. A letter and a packet of traveling money had brought him to Deerpole. It was the kind of money a man doesn't turn down without a very good reason. And he hadn't any. He'd just finished a job cutting a new trail down Wyoming way and he was happy to go north. He reached town a day early for his scheduled meeting with the man who had sent the letter, a J. B. Petersen, but he'd only been in town a little while when he felt he already knew something about the man. He was glad for that. It was always better than going into a meeting stone-cold.

It was late afternoon when he arrived in Deerpole and he let the magnificent Ovaro, with its pure white midsection and jet-black fore- and hindquarters, slowly walk through the town. The J. B. Petersen Saddlery was the first shop that took his eye. Next he saw the J. B. Petersen Stables and the J. B. Petersen Freight Warehouse. The J. B. Petersen Bank took up a corner near the center of town and another street away he saw the J. B. Petersen General Store. Maybe J. B. Petersen didn't own the whole town but he was sure a man of influence in it, Fargo concluded with quiet amusement. One of the only structures that didn't carry J. B. Petersen's name on it was the two-story frame house in the center of town that bore the sign:

DEERPOLE DANCEHALL
DOLLS & DRINKS

The town itself was ordinary enough, he saw, with perhaps a few more Owensboro mountain wagons and dead-axle drays than you'd find in most towns. But then Deerpole nestled alongside the Beaverhead range where any kind of hauling would require a mountain wagon with oversized brakes. He saw eyes turn to the Ovaro as he rode by, but that always happened in any town he entered. Dusk was beginning to slide across the land when he pulled the Ovaro to a halt in front of a two-story whitewashed building with the sign DEERPOLE INN over the front door. He tethered the horse to a hitching post and strode into the building. Three men lounged in chairs in what passed for a lobby. Two were half-asleep, hats perched on their heads; the third was a trim figure with a thatch of snow-white hair and very alert, gray eyes in a tanned and weathered face.

Fargo halted at the desk where a middle-aged man with horn-rimmed spectacles and a green eyeshade looked up at him. "Name's Fargo—Skye Fargo. I'm here for a meeting with J. B. Petersen," Fargo said. "Anybody come asking for me?"

"Nope," the clerk said.

"I was just wondering. I'm a day early," Fargo said.

"Then you can be sure nobody from Mr. Petersen's will be here till tomorrow," the desk clerk said, a hint of reproach in his tone.

"Stickler for time, is he?" Fargo remarked.

"Some folks call Mr. Petersen Mr. Precision," the clerk said. "Never to his face, of course."

"Then I'll enjoy a soft bed for the night," Fargo said and the clerk took a key from a row of others on wall pegs and handed it to him.

"Room three, down the hall. That'll be fifty cents," the man said. Fargo slipped the silver coin to him as he took the key and hurried outside to the Ovaro, pulled his saddle-bag and pack from the horse and returned to the inn. He walked down the corridor to the room, found it neat and clean with a single bed, a small table with a kerosene lamp on it, a straight-backed chair and a white-pine dresser with a big washbasin atop it. He set his things down, undressed and used the washbasin to freshen up and finally donned a clean shirt and strolled from the room.

The two half-asleep figures were still in the lobby but he found the white-haired man standing outside beside the Ovaro. He had a leanness to his trim figure that all but made one forget the thatch of white hair, Fargo decided. "That's a mighty fine-looking animal you have there," the man said admiringly.

"Thank you. That makes you a good judge of horseflesh." Fargo smiled.

"Been at it for enough years," the old man said.

"You as good a judge of a place to eat?" Fargo queried.

"At the dance hall, best food in town," the man answered. "And you can kill two birds with one stone."

Fargo's brows lifted. "Meaning what?" he asked.

"Meaning I didn't wait around just to compliment you on that Ovaro," the man said. "Been waiting for days for you to show up. I've a message for you."

"Who from?" Fargo frowned. "I don't know anybody in this town."

"From Evie. You can find her at the dance hall. She works there," the man said.

Fargo nodded. "Two birds with one stone," he said and it was the old man's turn to nod. "Who the hell is Evie?" Fargo frowned.

"Somebody who wants to see you," the old man said.

"You can do better than that," Fargo said.

The old man shrugged. "Not much," he said.

"What does Evie want with me?"

"That's for her to tell you."

"What does she look like?"

"Ask for Dolly. She runs the place. She'll point Evie out to you," the old man told him.

"What if I don't go? I'm not big on strange messages," Fargo said, his eyes hard on the old man.

"Then I've wasted three days waiting around," the man said.

"How did this Evie know I'd be coming into town?" Fargo pressed.

The old man half snorted, "Word gets around," he said. He was good with cryptic answers, Fargo grunted silently. But his curiosity had been aroused and he unwound the reins from the hitching post.

"As you said, I'm going over for a meal, anyway," he remarked.

"I'll walk over with you," the man said and fell into step beside Fargo.

"Where do you fit in?" Fargo questioned.

"I just carry messages," was the answer.

"Bullshit, friend," Fargo said blandly and the old man allowed a small shrug.

"I know Evie. We're old friends," he conceded.

"You've a name," Fargo said.

"Most folks call me Nugget."

"Old miner?"

"One who never struck it rich."

"You've plenty of company there," Fargo said and cast another glance at the man. His smallish, trim figure held together well but there were a myriad of tiny red veins in the weathered face that send their own message. "You mine for whiskey bottles now," he said and saw the man's quick glance of surprise.

"You judge a man real quick, Fargo," Nugget said.

"Usually real good," Fargo replied and drew a half-snort and nothing more until they reached the dance hall where a square stream of yellow light reached for the swinging doors into the night.

"You're on your own from here, Fargo," Nugget said.

"Afraid of temptation or afraid of being thrown out?" Fargo smiled.

"Some of both," the old man admitted wryly. "Good luck."

Fargo paused as he wondered how much the old man really knew. Or was he no more than he'd claimed to be, simply a messenger. "Where could I find you?" he asked.

"A shack, north end of town," the man said. "But you won't have any need to find me. Just talk to Evie."

"How come you and Evie are friends?" Fargo pressed.

Nugget shrugged as he thought for a moment. "Misery likes company, maybe," he said as he hurried away. Fargo turned and pushed his way through the two swinging doors into the dance hall. The usual scene of a long bar, smoke-filled air and round tables along three sides of the big room met his quick glance. And he saw the girls, in black-net tights, most of them with form-fitting satin tops, some dancing with patrons, others seated at the tables. They were the usual girls, grown old too quickly, every smile a mask. He moved foward, his eyes sweeping the dance hall again. A stairway led to the second floor at the back and he spotted a woman at a corner table near it—some thirty pounds overweight, part of it makeup and the jewelry that hung from her wrists and neck.

She had a round face with an extra chin, tightly curled bottle-blond hair and false eyelashes. But he saw none of the harshness in her face that many dance hall madams wore. Her eyes darted around the room more like a watchful mother hen than a taskmistress. Her eyes went to him as he strolled to her table, instant approval in her appraisal. "Hello, big man," she said in a throaty voice.

"You Dolly?" he asked.

"In person. What'll it be, drinks, dolls or both?" the woman asked.

"A good meal, first," Fargo said as he slid into a chair.

The woman snapped her fingers and one of the girls hastened over. "Bring the man a buffalo sandwich and lots of gravy," Dolly said.

"And a bourbon. No bar whiskey," Fargo added.

"You heard the man," Dolly said and Fargo watched the woman's eyes appraise him again. "I've some real nice girls for afterward," she said.

"I've one in mind," Fargo said and drew a glance of surprise.

"You've never been here before," Dolly said.

"That's right," Fargo said.

"Ah, somebody recommended a special girl," the woman said.

"Something like that." Fargo smiled. The strange message had surprised him. The old man had been cryptic. Fargo would keep things the same way for now. He exchanged small talk with the madam until the girl returned with his food and a bourbon. He sipped the whiskey. "Good," he said approvingly with a nod at the madam.

"Everything we have here is good, mister," she said. She sat back with a faintly amused smile toying with her lips until he finished the meal and downed the last of the bourbon. "Now who's this special girl you want?" she asked.

"Evie," he said and watched the woman's plucked eyebrows shoot upward.

"Evie?" she echoed, disbelief in her voice.

"That so surprising?" Fargo questioned.

"It sure as hell is, especially from a handsome gent like you," the madam said. "Evie's only been here for a few weeks and nobody's taken to her. She's just not the type for this kind of work. I told her so."

"Why'd you take her on?"

"Because I'm a sucker for stray cats," the woman said. "There was some big breakup with a boyfriend who took off. Then she was fired from her job at the general store. Some of my girls knew her from there."

"And told her to come to you for a job," Fargo said.

"She seemed awfully nervous and afraid when she came. I think she was looking for any place to feel safe. I told her

I'd take her on trial. I knew she wasn't going to work out."

"But you felt sorry for her," Fargo said.

"I told you, I'm a sucker for stray cats," the woman said.

"I've heard of worse things to be," Fargo replied and let his eyes move across the room. "Which one is she?" he asked.

"She's upstairs. I keep her there till later," Dolly said.

"Why?"

"The customers. The more they drink the less particular they are," she said and Fargo smiled. "You think I'm being callous," she said.

"Nobody's perfect," Fargo said. "You have the right. Is she that bad?"

"No, she's just not the kind my customers take to," the madam said, paused and Fargo saw her eyes narrow at him. "Then you're not my average customer. Nobody recommended her to you. Something else brought you here looking for her," she said.

"Maybe." He shrugged and the woman gave a little grunt, pleased with herself. She called another of the girls over.

"Go and tell Evie to come down here," she said and the girl hurried to the stairs as Fargo sat back. Dolly exchanged banter with a few passing patrons while Fargo's eyes stayed on the stairs. He had no need to question Dolly when the girl came down the stairs. She wore the black-net stockings all the other girls wore but she was slightly built, her red satin top covering plainly small breasts. He watched her approach him, her eyes round, a light blue. She had a wan, waiflike quality to her that evoked instant protectiveness.

"Nugget sent me," he murmured softly and her round eyes grew rounder.

"You're Fargo," she said and he nodded. "Come upstairs with me," she said and he rose as she turned. He cast a glance at Dolly and saw the woman watching him with uncertainty.

He threw her a smile. "One more good deed," he said and she tossed a glance of grim patience back. But she turned away and he laughed softly as he followed the girl up the stairs. Dolly had a good heart under all that paint and powder, he murmured to himself. He reached the upstairs corridor just a step behind Evie and saw a dim passageway with kerosene lamps shaded by deep-red glass to make the hall even dimmer. Evie halted at a door near the end of the corridor, opened it and admitted him to a small room all but filled by a big bed and a straight-backed chair. A narrow bureau took up the only remaining wall space.

A lamp turned low offered a dim, yellow glow as Evie sat down on the edge of the bed. "Thanks for coming," she said in a small, thin voice that matched her waiflike quality. He wanted to be brusque and annoyed. He'd every reason to be, he told himself, yet he couldn't manage it. With no attempt to manipulate, she had a disarming air to her, he realized.

"What's this all about, Evie?" he asked gently.

"It's about a favor I'm asking," she said. "I know why you're here. I don't want you to kill Burt."

Fargo frowned at her. "I'm here because I got a letter about a job," he said.

The girl's smooth forehead creased. "That's all you know?" she asked.

"Yes, that's all," Fargo snapped. "Maybe you should tell me the rest, seeing as you seem to know so much."

She frowned in thought for a moment. "I don't know if I should," she said. "Anyway, I want to talk about our agreement, first."

"About my not killing Burt?"

"That's right," she nodded.

"First, who's Burt?" she asked.

"He was my boyfriend."

"The one who ran away," Fargo said and saw the surprise flash in her pale blue eyes. "Dolly mentioned it," he added.

"He had to run," the girl said.

"Why would I want to kill him?" Fargo questioned.

"It might just happen and I don't want that, so I want to make our bargain first," Evie said.

"Such as?"

"I'll pay you not to kill Burt. Only I don't have any money right now," she said. "You can have me, instead. Now, tomorrow, when you come back—anytime, anywhere, as often as you like."

She halted, waited and he studied her wan face that had suddenly taken on a determination that seemed out of place in it. "Burt must be quite a guy," Fargo said.

She offered a wry smile. "I may never see him again but he was good to me when I needed someone. He did a lot for me. Now it's my turn. That's the way I am."

Fargo's smile was gentle as he continued to study her. "Maybe you're quite a young woman," he said, words that were more than a glib compliment. There was a quiet strength behind her waiflike air.

She returned a shrug. "It's something I want to do," she said and her pale blue eyes focused on him as he continued to study her and she suddenly rose to her feet. "Maybe I'm not all that beautiful but you'll enjoy it, I promise," she said, a touch of defensiveness in her voice.

"Wasn't thinking about that," Fargo said.

"You were thinking about something," Evie said.

"I was thinking I'd best find out more about why I'm here and how it involves your friend, Burt," Fargo said.

"He'd be a side issue, but he could still get killed and that's what I don't want to happen," Evie said.

"Maybe I can see that that doesn't happen. I don't know. I don't know much of anything. But there'll be no bargaining with you for it," Fargo said.

The tiny furrow moved across her smooth forehead as she fastened him with a sidelong glance filled with skepticism. "You saying you'd do what I want with nothing between us?" she rephrased.

"Guess so," he grunted.

"Why?" Evie asked, the furrow deepening.

He shrugged. "That's the way I feel. Consider it a present. Everybody makes their own choices about what's right and what's wrong."

The furrow became a full frown. "No, I wouldn't ask that. It wouldn't be fair," she said.

"Don't look a gift horse in the mouth, honey," he said.

"No, it'd be wrong. I've my own ideas about what's right and what's wrong. We make a bargain and seal it here and now. I want an agreement, not charity," Evie said firmly.

Fargo's lips tightened in a grim half-smile. She had her own stubborn integrity. Maybe it was skewed, but it was there and she'd cling to it, he realized. Once again, another facet of her waiflike appeal reached out. "One condition," he said. "You tell me everything you know about why I'm here."

"All right, but afterward. We seal it first. I don't want you changing your mind," she said.

"How do you know I won't do that anyway, afterward?" he slid at her.

"You won't do that. You're not that kind. I can tell," she said.

"You that good a judge of men?" He laughed.

"Inside things," she said with a lofty simplicity that he understood all too well. She took a step backward, unsnapped the buttons at the bottom of her red top, slid the black-net stockings from her legs with graceful, quick motions and then undid another pair of hooks and the top fell from her. She stood before him with a kind of defiant pride, as if daring him to disparage her with a glance or expression. He'd no mind to do that, anyway, but she would have pushed it aside if he'd had the urge. The waiflike quality in her face echoed faintly in her body, yet she had a surprising sensuality. His eyes moved down a slim, girlish form with small breasts, slightly flat, tipped by tiny pink nipples.

She had a lean, trim body, small-waisted, good hips and a flat belly and just beneath it, a surprisingly full, thick black nap. Her legs, on the thin side, still kept a shape with thighs that were long and inviting. She sat down on the bed, lay back on her elbows and the pale blue eyes shone with a tiny flickering fire. She was, he decided, a strange combination of waif and wanton hussy—little-girl appeal and very womanly sensuality, contrasts both physical and emotional. Her flat little breasts somehow managed to turn up as she lay waiting. She drew one leg up with slow provocativeness.

He undid his gunbelt, let it slide to the floor and followed with his clothes as he felt himself already responding to her. When he stood naked before her, he saw her eyes fasten on him and the tiny flicker suddenly grew into a pale fire. He lowered himself atop her gently. She was small to the touch, his hand almost encompassing her ribs on one side, but he felt her body quiver as their skins met. "What if I'd been a fat, ugly old fossil?" he asked. "Would you still have gone through with it?"

"I don't know. That honest enough for you?" she answered and he nodded. "Probably," she added. "But I'd have hated everything about it."

"And now?"

"I don't think I'm going to hate anything," Evie murmured. Her mouth opened for his lips and he felt her thin arms come up to wrap around his neck. Her tongue was quick, darting out to meet his, her mouth softly drawing him in and she murmured a sigh. His hands found one small breast and gently caressed the tiny pink tip, felt it harden and grow a fraction higher. He pulled his mouth from hers, drew his lips down her neck to the other breast and pulled all of it into his oral embrace. He let his tongue circle the tiny tip and Evie's little murmur grew stronger, becoming a thin cry of delight. He felt her body move, half-twist one way, then the other, stretch itself out and he let his hand slide down over the flat abdomen and push into the thick nap. He closed his fingers gently in the denseness, the soft filaments wrapping around his fingers as he massaged the little Venus mound. "Yes, Jesus, yes. . . ." Evie whispered and again he felt her body stretch out.

Her hips lifted, her small frame suddenly finding a wiry strength as he felt her thighs grow muscled. His hand slipped from the dense black nap, smoothed the flesh of her lean thighs and moved upward, cupping around the moist and secret place. Evie gave a short cry of delight as he touched deeper. Her hands made fluttery little motions along his back, little exhortations of touch and her hips rose in a tiny, bouncing movement. Her thin body half-twisted again and the small, flat breasts moved from side to side. He felt himself responding and her hands were against his buttocks, pulling him atop her. She gave a little cry as his throbbing member came against the dense nap. "Yes, yes, Jesus, yes . . ." she gasped out as her thighs fell wide apart and she repeated the tiny, bouncing motion with her hips.

He was just bringing himself to her waiting openness when he heard the loud snap of the door being flung open, crashing against the wall, the sound as jarring as it was unexpected. Still atop Evie, about to slide forward to her, he turned his head to see three men burst into the room, all with six-guns in their hands. His own gun lay on the floor between the bed and the intruders, too far away to reach without being blasted, he saw. There was a narrow space between the other side of the bed and the wall, hardly more than a foot and a half. He rolled from atop Evie, flung himself into the space as with one hand he yanked her with him. He had her almost pulled into the space when the trio opened fire.

"Aw, shit," Fargo groaned as he felt Evie's body shudder as the shots thudded into her. "Goddamn sonofabitches," he shouted as he rose, fury throwing aside prudence. Two more bullets slammed into Evie. Fargo dived across the bed, hit the other side and somersaulted to the floor. He had his hand on the Colt as the three men turned and began to streak for the door. He got the gun up fast enough to fire one shot at the last of the three figures, saw the man clutch at the back of his leg before he disappeared from sight.

Fargo leaped to his feet, raced forward to see the man dragging himself into the corridor. "Freeze," he shouted and saw the man turn and bring his gun up. Fargo fired and this time the man clutched at his midsection as he flew backward and hit the wall. Fargo ran past his body as it slid to the floor. The other two were almost to the end of the corridor. One of the two looked back for an instant. "Down the stairs, Jack," he said, words clipped out with an accent that was German or maybe Swedish.

"I'm goin'," the other said in a very throaty, husky voice. Both disappeared down the stairs as Fargo raced forward, hit the top step and leaped down the next three and the three that followed. He heard the rising shouts of alarm as the main room of the dance hall appeared in front of him. Customers and girls ducked and flattened themselves on the floor as the two gun-waving figures raced across the room. "Out of the way, goddammit," the one shouted in his throaty voice. Fargo cursed as he aimed the Colt. A fat man got in the way as he drew a bead on the man with the accent. He shifted his aim to the other one.

"Damn," he swore as he aimed the gun and fired just as the men reached the doorway. His shot sent a shower of wood splinters from the door. Both men raced out of the dance hall and Fargo lowered the Colt. He saw the madam huddled in one corner staring up at him. So were all the other eyes in the room and it was only then that he realized he was stark naked. He retreated up the stairs, turned and ran back to the room where he swore softly as he dived onto the bed and reached down to pull Evie from the narrow space. He had felt the bullets thud into her thin body and he'd held no hopes for a miracle but he swore again as he found himself too right. He held Evie's small form in his arms, rocked her for a long moment before he put her down on the bed.

He rose, his chest covered with blood from her wounds. He had just drawn on his trousers when Dolly came into the room, followed by the bartender and a man with a sheriff's badge on his vest. She looked down at Evie and he heard her sob. "Oh, God," she breathed and brought her gaze up to Fargo's bitter, angry eyes. "What happened?"

"You tell me," he bit out. "Didn't you see them go by you, dammit?"

"I saw them go upstairs. I didn't think anything of it. Sometimes the girls make arrangements they tell me about later. Then I heard the shooting," Dolly said. "Evie didn't have any enemies. They had to be after you."

"I figured that out myself," Fargo snapped. "I just don't know why."

"What's your name, mister?" the man with the badge said. "I'm Sheriff Hood."

"Fargo, Skye Fargo. I came for a meeting with J. B. Petersen."

"You're the one," the sheriff grunted.

"Jesus, everybody in this town knows about me coming here?" Fargo asked.

"Wouldn't say everybody but there's been talk," the sheriff said.

"Enough to have three hired-guns come after me," Fargo threw back bitterly. "And I don't know a damn reason why."

"I don't know that, either, mister," the man said.

"But I'll bet you could take a guess," Fargo probed.

"I don't gamble and I don't guess," the sheriff said and leaned out into the corridor. "I'll send Jake to haul this one away," he said to Dolly as he left.

The woman turned to Fargo. "I'll see to Evie. Hell, you

just met her. It's my place to take care of things," she said.

"A man gave me her message to come see her. Called himself Nugget. Seems they were friends," Fargo said.

"Yes, old Nugget. I'll see that he hears, though somebody will tell him before I do," Dolly said with another quick glance at the bed. "I'll take care of her real proper, Fargo," she said.

He reached into his pocket and handed her a dozen bills. "Get her a real headstone," he said.

Dolly nodded. "I'll send a girl with water and towels for you," she said and hurried from the room. He lowered himself to the edge of the bed beside the small, still form and his hand was still stroking her hair when the girl arrived with the towels and a large washbasin. She helped him clean himself off before he put on the rest of his clothes.

The saloon was a strangely subdued place when he went downstairs, half the customers gone. He strode out into the night. His lips were a thin line as he unhitched the Ovaro. It had become damn obvious that the offer that had brought him here to Deerpole had all kinds of dirty strings attached to it. And too many people knew about those strings. He couldn't claim anything so profound as betrayal. He couldn't even claim he'd been misled. The letter had neither promised nor implied. But he had just been damn near killed and that deserved an answer. And a young woman lay dead and she deserved justice.

J. B. Petersen was suddenly more than a name at the bottom of a letter in his pocket. It was a question mark that needed answers. With cold anger seething inside him, he climbed onto the Ovaro. He'd paid for a room and a soft bed at the inn. But he had been trailed to Evie. Maybe others were laying in wait at the Inn. He decided not to risk another dry-gulching. He could pick up his things in the morning. He turned the horse south and rode from town, and climbed a low hill until he found the big cottonwood. Now he turned off his thoughts and closed his eyes.

Evie's slender form and sweet, wan face drifted through his mind. Hell, he'd never even learned her last name, he realized. He went to sleep wrapped in grim anger he knew would be no less grim when the new day dawned.